VOW TO RESPECT

A FLYING CROSS RANCH ROMANCE
BOOK FIVE

SHANAE JOHNSON

THOSE JOHNSON GIRLS

CHAPTER ONE

"Even though scissors are a part of the art program, I can't do my job if you keep cutting the funding."

Kailyn Jade resisted the urge to grab the sharp pair of scissors sitting in the organizer on the large oak desk. The office supply sat blade side up, far too dangerous to be in a classroom. But she wasn't in a classroom just now. She was in the assistant principal's office.

Owen Sharp's smirk was razor-edged, like his name and the unsafe display on his desk. His blond hair spiked up to the ceiling, likely in an effort to get away from whatever thoughts were going on in that delusional brain of his.

"Your funding hasn't been cut, sweetheart," he said.

Kailyn resisted the urge to go up onto her tiptoes as she faced off against her nemesis. He wasn't truly her nemesis. He was worse. He was her boss. And her ex-boyfriend. Kinda. Sorta. She didn't think their two dates counted, but he surely did.

"It hasn't grown," Kailyn said. "And don't call me sweetheart."

"You used to like it when I called you sweetheart."

That had been a major part of the reason she hadn't accepted a third date from him. Kailyn had never liked being called sweetheart. Just as she had never liked being called cutie. Or shortie. Or worse, red.

As if it heard itself being talked about, one of her red curls escaped her headband and bounced in front of her eyes. Kailyn reached up to swipe the lock away, but another vision of red danced in her eyes. This time, the color was on her index finger.

The red paint she'd been using in her art classroom to help guide Chad Martin through his feelings of anxiety over his parents separating was smeared from her fingertip to her knuckle. There were splashes of green and white from helping Lynnette Hardy find the perfect shade of green to express her feelings of her two best friends going on a shopping trip without her. And then, of course, there was the rainbow of colors on Kailyn's smock from her six periods of classes today. The smock was supposed to keep the paint off her clothes, but Kailyn had long since given up the battle to keep any of her wardrobe paint-free.

From the first moment she'd picked up a crayon as a toddler, Kailyn had found her calling. Even when she had been scolded by her foster parents for drawing on the walls, she hadn't been deterred. She had been terrified that they would send her and her sister back to the foster care home. Instead, they handed her a sponge to clean up her mess. By the time she was done, her foster dad had gone to the store and brought back an easel and a handful of canvases.

"You could let me call you sweetheart again," Owen was saying, "and I'll see what I can—"

Kailyn made a disgusted sound in the back of her throat. This was the other reason why they'd broken up. Everything was always tit for tat with him. And she was usually the one giving both and receiving little in return. That was not how relationships were meant to go.

Not that she believed things could ever truly be equal between two people. Someone would always give a little more than the other with such fluctuating math. Just the thought of an equation to try and balance out a healthy relationship made the left side of her brain hurt.

"You're sending more money to the sports program than others," she said.

Now there was math she could manage. Kailyn had had a look at the balance sheet for the supplies for the day as well as the after-school programs. When the spreadsheet was ordered from greatest to least, the art program was at the very bottom of the list. Unfortunately, that math hadn't changed in the three years she'd been working at the school.

"The sports programs bring in revenue," Owen countered.

"Art may not pay in dollars, but it does pay in sense. Kids are experiencing more and more mental health issues these days. Art is a proven way to deal with those emotions that they don't know how to process. An art therapy after school program is an investment in their futures."

"What future? You'd be a struggling artist if you weren't an art teacher."

Kailyn had long since given up counting to ten with Owen. On their first date, she'd counted to ten three times. On their second, she'd gotten as far as a hundred before the main course was finished. Trying for patience with Owen didn't work. Which made her wonder how a man who was in charge of hormone-riddled teenagers at the high school kept his job as the chief disciplinarian.

"I might be a struggling artist," she said, "but I'm a happy, well-adjusted and whole person because I'm in touch with my emotions."

A bell rang from overhead, causing Kailyn's shoulders to bunch. A second later, the sound of yelling and screaming bounced off the walls. The squeak of tennis shoes pounding against linoleum made her eye twitch. The change between periods was her least favorite time of day, topped only by the end of school when all of the children made a beeline for their lockers and milled around for longer than the five minutes of break between classes.

As an artist, Kailyn appreciated the artistry of chaos. But only on a canvas where it could be contained by a frame. Emotions were at their most effective when they could be captured by a pencil or paintbrush. Which was why she not only wanted more supplies for her classroom, but an after-school art therapy program for more kids to express themselves in a quiet and methodical way.

"These are teenagers," Owen was saying. "All they have are out-of-control feelings."

"Art therapy can help channel those feelings for a productive use."

"Look, sweet—"

The look on Kailyn's face made Owen begin again. He was still under the delusion that they were on a break and would get back together. That break would last until the end of time, as far as she was concerned.

"I would give you the funds if I could," he continued. "But the school board is in charge of after school funding."

That was new. The vice principals were usually in charge of recreational programming for schools.

"It's a new rule because they want to make sure things are done fairly," Owen said. "They're looking at two programs. Yours is one. You'll need to make a presentation to them next week."

This was great. She was great at presentations. It used her artistic skill to make beautiful posterboards and slides to bring her vision to life. The right side of her brain was eager to get to work. It was the left side of her brain that was held back with some anxiety.

She knew she could make a presentation pretty. However, when she spoke to people about the tenants of art therapy, few, if any, took to the idea. Just as many people had hang-ups about going to a mental health therapist, and they were even less willing to work out their issues with a paint brush and palette.

"I could put in a good word for you."

Kailyn wasn't interested in Owen's words, good or bad. There was only one person's advice she could rely on in a matter such as this. Leaving the administrative suite, she walked across the hall to the guidance counselors' office.

Passing by the first open door in the counselor's wing, she smiled at Mr. Fox, who had been counseling kids on career and college since she'd gone here. She avoided the shrewd gaze of Ms. Ayala, the academic counselor who had been hired in Kailyn's last year at the school when her grades had started to slip. At the third open door, Kailyn peered in and saw a mirror image of herself.

Elayne had the same deep, reddish-brown

auburn hair as Kailyn. But where Kailyn let her curls bounce free, only confined by a headband to leave her eyes unobstructed, Elayne had her hair pulled back in a severe bun. Her twin sister held up her finger with one hand while she cradled the phone in the other.

"I'm looking forward to it, Dr. Patel," she said into the phone receiver. "I have no doubt your program on trauma in children is going to help me in working with students in our community."

Elayne was headed to a conference for school guidance counselors and social workers hosted by the Purple Heart Ranch, which was a rehabilitation ranch for soldiers. In the last few years, the ranch had also begun an after-school and summer program for the town's youth. They were doing remarkable work with children from disadvantaged and low-income homes.

Closing the door to her sister's office, Kailyn looked around at the pictures on the wall of her and her sister as kids, in college, with their foster parents, and at the camps where they'd worked. The twins were a dynamic duo. Where Kailyn got kids to express their feelings, Elayne was excellent at helping them to focus that released energy into something productive.

"Good news," Kailyn said when her sister hung up the phone.

"Bad news," Elayne said at the same time.

"You go first," said Kailyn.

"You'll never guess who's back in town."

Honor Valley was a small town. Not exactly a town where everyone knew everyone else. More of a town where everyone knew *of* everyone else. But even that distinction belonged to the older generation. Many of the second and third generations had left for bigger cities and broader opportunities.

"Who?" asked Kailyn.

"The Terrible Twins."

Kailyn's heart stopped. There were three sets of twins in the valley. The Silver sisters were bossy girls, but they had never been terrible to either Kailyn or Elayne. Besides, Tilly and Gunny had been back for months and were both happily married and settled. That left the other two.

"Maybe they're just visiting?" asked Kailyn, her voice sounding breathless.

"We can only hope. This town isn't big enough for Jades and Matthews."

The notion of Aldo and Mateo Matthews brought Kailyn mixed feelings. Both emotions resided in the pit of her stomach. The thought of Aldo made her feel sick. The thought of Mateo…

Kailyn was supposed to hate Mateo Matthews.

And she did.

Well, she disliked him.

Just not when she thought of his face. Because every time she saw his handsome face, he offered her a smile. It was a smile that stopped her heart each time. No man had ever done that since him.

Which was all the reason to hate him even more.

"They're both still enlisted. They're probably just on leave visiting their father." As soon as the words were out of Kailyn's mouth, she winced. She didn't want her sister to think she was keeping tabs on the twins.

"If they are visiting, hopefully it's just for a few days, and they'll be gone by the time I get back," Elayne huffed, brushing back a nonexistent wayward strand of hair. "What's your good news?"

It took Kailyn a moment to think before she remembered. "The art therapy program is as good as mine, but I'm going to need your help."

CHAPTER TWO

"It's all but a done deal, son."

Mateo Matthews clasped hands with General Alan Jensen. Though the older man had a head full of white hair, it was clear he still kept up with his Basic Training regimen. His biceps were nearly as big as Mateo's head. In fact, Mateo had to stop himself from wincing at the strength of General Jensen's grip on his right hand.

The general had recruited most of Mateo's brothers. The man was as old as his father, but he still looked half his age. That's one thing military training did for you. If you kept up the regiments, it kept your body in top shape.

"Thank you, sir." Even if Mateo had not been a member of the Armed Forces for the last eight years, his parents had drilled manners and etiquette into him from a tender age.

"No, thank you, Captain Matthews."

General Jensen gave one more affirmative shake of Mateo's hand before letting go. Mateo's knuckles snapped, crackled, and popped back into place now that they'd regained their freedom. "Will I need to talk to anyone else from the school board? The principal, perhaps?"

"It's the board that makes these decisions. Something or other about fairness and equality of all programs." General Jensen shrugged.

Though the United States Military served an entirely democratic society, the organization itself had a strict hierarchal structure. A soldier always knew their place in a room according to the rank that they'd earned.

"What you're planning to do will be invaluable to this community," said General Jensen. "It will give the youth an outlet for their energy and a purpose for their future."

Mateo agreed. As a youth, he'd had more energy than could be contained in his small body. Growing up in the foster care system, it was prudent to be seen and not heard, and never seen to be doing anything too boisterous if you wanted to get adopted. Unfortunately, it was too much to ask for growing boys to sit still and keep quiet. It had taken a saint to adopt not only him, but his brother as well.

Haran Matthews and his wife Tessa had taken in six boys when they were already past their own childbearing years. The Matthews had made him into a good person, but it was the Air Force that had made Mateo into a man. Now Mateo wanted to provide other young boys and girls with the same opportunity. The JROTC program he'd proposed to General Jensen would provide the kids of Honor Valley a launch pad for that life.

Originally, when Mateo had made his plans to retire from the Air Force and come home to the valley, he'd planned to work with the Bright Horizons Foster Home, the place that had taken in him and his brother when they had nowhere to go. Now that place was situated on his foster dad's homestead. He would continue to lend a hand there, but he wanted a project that was all his own.

"I have the ear of the board," General Jensen was saying. "One word from me and the funding for an after-school JROTC program is yours. There isn't any viable competition."

The general held out his hand again. Mateo

masked his face before he grimaced at another of the ultra-firm handshakes. If this was the only hardship he'd face on his way to his bright new future, then he had absolutely nothing to complain about.

He slipped his hand into Jensen's and took the brunt of the assault. The second wasn't so bad now that he was prepared for it. When the general let his hand go, Mateo felt a sense of peace wash over him. A handshake was as good as a man's word. First, his birth father had taught him that. Then his foster father had reinforced the lesson.

"The board meets next Monday," said the general. "We'll make it formal then."

With a nod, the man walked off. His gait was the powerful stride of a man who'd spent more than half his life in the military. Before General Jensen turned the corner, he nodded as another man saluted him. Once the general was out of sight, the other man strode purposefully to Mateo.

Looking the newcomer up and down, Mateo couldn't help but let out a long, low sigh. When he'd gotten up this morning, he'd done so as quietly as possible so as not to wake his sleeping brother. The two were sharing the pull-out couch in the family room at the Flying Cross Ranch.

Their family home was overflowing with all of the Matthews boys home as well as the five foster kids taking up residence in the boys' old bunkhouse.

Mateo had offered to sleep at a hotel. None of his family would hear of it. The most vocal naysayer was his brother, who was walking toward him.

Even though Aldo had been fast asleep when Mateo had crept out of the family room before dawn, his twin had managed to pull on the same gray shirt and jeans that Mateo was wearing. The only differentiating visual between them was the shoes they wore. Mateo wore cowboy boots, where Aldo had pulled on black military boots.

"There you are," Aldo grumped. "I've been looking all over for you."

"I told you I had to come into town for a meeting."

"You should've woken me up so we could come together."

But that was just it. They weren't doing this project together. Mateo wouldn't mind if they stopped doing a lot of things together. Especially the dressing alike part.

Mateo had put up with it when his birth mother had dressed them alike. Though she'd done it mostly because she bought their discount clothing in bulk. Mateo would have done anything in the world to earn one of his mother's smiles. So when it came time to dress each morning, he dutifully put on what she laid out for her twin boys without any protest.

He still remembered the outfit she'd chosen for her sons as well as her husband on the day of their citizenship ceremony. He had been proud to dress like his father. Mateo still remembered the pride in his father's eyes as he peered back at his family as he recited his vows to the country of his heart. His mother had cried. It was the first time Mateo had understood happy tears and the word oxymoron.

Just a few months later, his parents would be taken away from them by someone breaking the rules. A drunk driver would take their precious lives and leave Mateo and his brother with no one. Into the foster system they'd went.

After they were adopted by the Matthews, Mateo wanted nothing more than his own individuality. He often tried to sneak out before Aldo woke and insisted they wore the same thing. All it would take was his younger brother's—younger by ten minutes —lip to start quivering and Mateo would give in.

Now that the twins were no longer children, and no longer in the military, there was no good reason for them to dress alike. Or do much else alike either.

"You're really doing this?" said Aldo. "You're going to work with runts?"

"We used to be runts."

"That's the benefit of growing up. We don't have to deal with runts anymore."

Mateo not only wanted to deal with other people's runts, he wanted to deal with his own runts. The problem was there was only one girl he could see himself making runts with. He had an uphill battle where she was concerned.

"You don't have to deal with the JROTC program," said Mateo. "You can sign your contract and reenlist."

"Without you?" Aldo scrunched up his nose.

The scrunching was a familiar expression. When Aldo had decided he didn't like olives, he frowned, scrunching up his nose at Mateo every time he popped one into his mouth. He even went so far as to feign sickness whenever Mateo dared to enjoy the offensive fruit.

Aldo also insisted that they have the same friends. As well as the same enemies. That last one had been an anchor around Mateo's ankles for far too long.

"We're going to live our own lives from now," Mateo said. "My life is going to be here."

Aldo shrugged. "I'm not in a rush to sign a new contract. I can stay home. For a while."

Mateo pinched the bridge of his nose. His brother had selective hearing. At least their shoes were different today. It was a start. Now he just had to figure out how to ditch his brother long enough to go in search of a particular girl with dark red curls that made his heart skip a beat.

"Topher told me there are private military contractors visiting the Purple Heart Ranch this week," said Aldo. "With so many soldiers recuperating there, it's like fertile ground for the picking."

Well, that would be good. A few days on his own without his twin dogging his steps. A lot could happen in a few days.

CHAPTER THREE

ailyn closed the door to her sister's office with a quiet snick. Checking in with her twin had been just the right idea to help her get started on the presentation for the board. Though she and Elayne had shared a womb, it might have been better if they'd burst into the world sharing a brain. Where Kailyn was clearly a right-brained person, artistic, creative, emotional, her sister's head listed to the left where logic resided.

Elayne was far more balanced than Kailyn. She could quickly analyze a situation and had the capacity to deal with both logistic and emotional fallout. It was a feat Kailyn both admired and begrudged.

Elayne always offered her more well-rounded brain to Kailyn whenever she asked. When it came to anything artistic, Elayne was all thumbs. They never attempted the switching places cliché everyone always thought twins got up to. Instead, they asked the other for help where they were weak. One weakness that Kailyn had never asked her sister's advice or guidance on was Mateo Matthews.

Walking the halls of the school, Kailyn saw the ghost of Mateo Matthews in Mrs. Cristobel's doorway, where he'd always leave with a smile. Mateo had been good at math. Whenever he raised his hand to give the answer, he always explained how he'd arrived at the solution. The lightbulb would go off over Kailyn's head each time he did, and she'd finally understand how to do that problem and then the next.

Next, she saw the ghost of his muscular teenage form bent over the water fountain after football practice. He was always there at that particular water fountain, which was right outside the art room, even though the boys' locker room and the football field were on the other side of the school. But she supposed it was the least crowded of drinking fountains, and that had to be why he always used it and ran the risk of running late to practice.

She also had a clear memory of Mateo sitting in the center of the cafeteria, where she would always sit on the fringe or take her meals in the art room. Like hers, Mateo's plate was always piled high with cafeteria food, even snagging the uneaten portions of their friends' before they could place the unopened cartoons of milk or fruit cups in the trash. She'd see him again at the end of the lunch period, placing his empty tray on the rack before leaving.

Kailyn understood that sentiment as a foster kid. Even though they both had been adopted by the time they were in high school, and they were in stable homes with good people, abandoned kids remembered the feeling of always being hungry. It never truly went away.

What was always a part of her memory, and never a ghost, was the vivid sparkle in his hazel eyes whenever he'd catch sight of her. Sometimes, when they were alone in the halls, he would smile at her. That smile always made her feet miss a step and her heart skip a beat.

It was cruel, that smile. Cruel because she could not return it. Not when he stood by as his brother, who never missed an opportunity to verbally assault her sister. Not when she walked side by side with her sister, who Kailyn was sure would claw out Aldo Matthew's eyes if given half the chance.

Kailyn never knew the reason Aldo had taken such a dislike to Elayne. Her sister had never been able to fully articulate why she hated Aldo so fiercely. They both must have sprung into the world this way and would go out swinging at each other in their elder years.

In the meantime, whenever they met, Elayne and Aldo would lay waste to everything in their path. They'd suck the color out of the day with their snips and snipes. If they remained too long in the same vicinity, the world would surely combust under their deep-seated hatred of one another.

Which was why it was such a blessing when the Matthews twins flew away to join the Air Force. There had been peace in the valley for eight years. There also hadn't been anyone else who had smiled at Kailyn in the way that made her miss a step or her heart skip a beat.

"Girls cook, not boys. So what does that make you?"

For a moment, Kailyn froze. It was more the

tone than the actual words. There was the sound of a sneer in the speaker's tone. Whenever Aldo spoke to Elayne, he always wrinkled his nose, which made the pitch of his deep voice go an octave higher. To this day, if anyone spoke to Kailyn while wrinkling their nose, her shoulders would huddle in on herself and she'd go mute while her sister confronted her bully, making both her five-foot-four stature appear bigger and her light voice go gruffer.

Whomever was being sneered at didn't growl. They spoke in a friendly tone. "Actually, a majority of chefs are males. It's very sexist if you think about it, and I'm a feminist."

Kailyn picked up her steps again. Her light footfalls were the only thing that could be heard in the stunned silence. She peered around the corner, and standing in front of Mateo's water fountain was a group of four boys.

Though group was the wrong word. There was a pack of three who stood together. Those three faced off against one smaller boy. The smaller boy smiled up at the predators. Of all things, he held a cloche in his hands. He clearly didn't realize he was prey and would soon be served up.

"Oh look, guys, this little feminist made cookies in her Easy Bake Oven."

"The Easy Bake Oven packets are special formulas." The little chef shook his head in an admonishing factor, still not getting the fact that he was in danger. "I made these from scratch with—"

The chef didn't get to finish his recipe. One of the pack smacked the cloche from his hands. The dish fell to the floor. Some of the cupcakes fell into the inside of the cloche's dome. Others fell with a splat—icing side down—on the linoleum floor.

Kailyn hated confrontations. She hated any type of fighting. But even more, she hated watching anyone get picked on. So why had she chosen to work in a high school where bullying ran rampant? Well, it was the only job available to her at the time.

Most of the time, she preferred to stay inside her classroom with her peaceful art supplies. There were few arguments or fights here in this wing of the school where the theater and band department were housed. But every once in a while, something went down.

Usually, another teacher was nearby to stop it. Right now, Kailyn was the only adult in sight. She picked up her steps to get to the fray, but someone beat her to it.

"Knock it off before I make you eat that off the floor."

A tall, skinny kid placed himself at the center of the confrontation. He had an inch or two on the boys in the pack, but he was outnumbered. His thin body stood protectively in front of the little chef.

"Chill, Denny," said the kid that must have been the pack leader. "We're just joking."

"We gotta get home anyway," said his packmate to the left. "My mom baked us cookies."

The packmate on the right sneered, picking up the new line of insults. "I'm heading home to play catch with my dad."

The pack leader affected a false frown. "These two wouldn't know anything about that."

The words were a physical punch to Denny, to the little chef, and to Kailyn. She'd had mean girls pull the same kind of thing with her in school when they learned she was a foster child. Kids were cruel, and they were often cruelest to the poor and the parentless.

"You three are not going home," said the voice of an adult. Kailyn was surprised to find that adult had the same pitch as her own voice. She opened her mouth to continue. "Not until you go to the janitor's closet, clean this mess up, and then wait for me to call your parents to let them know what you did here."

The young wolves' jaws twitched. Their claw-less fingers clenched. For a moment, Kailyn wasn't a teacher. She wasn't an adult. She was a little girl facing off against bullies again.

"If I repeat myself, it'll be a week of detention with the other Ms. Jade added on top."

That got the pack in motion. "Yes, Ms. Jade," they intoned.

Whereas Kailyn had a reputation for being soft, everyone knew Elayne was hardcore. Many students were seen leaving her office in tears. The threat of going into the guidance office and talking about their feelings was enough to turn most boys green.

Kailyn watched as the three walked down the hall to the janitor's closet. When she turned back to the other two, she wasn't met with thanks and praise. They weren't regarding her at all. They were in a tense argument.

"You can't be a pushover, Miguel. You have to fight back."

"I'm not a fighter. I offered them cupcakes. Here." Miguel picked up a cupcake that had rolled inside the cloche. "You can have this one."

Denny rolled his eyes and stormed off without the cupcake—or any acknowledgement of Kailyn.

Miguel looked up at Kailyn as she approached. He held the treat out to her. The cake bottom was a deep red. The icing was a creamy white. Sprinkles were artfully placed around the top like a starburst.

"Thank you, ma'am."

Kailyn winced at the ma'am. But it showed the kid had manners. Whoever was fostering this kid was doing right by him.

"This looks beautiful—Miguel, is it?"

He nodded. "I was trying to mimic Van Gogh's *Starry Night*."

"I see it." Kailyn grinned as she admired the artistic flair. "You're a foster kid?"

Shame spread across Miguel's cheeks, much like the pattern on his cupcake.

"I was, too."

"I used to horde food. Now I share." Miguel shrugged. "I thought I was evolving."

Kailyn liked this kid immensely. He was far more evolved than the pack animals lugging brooms and a mop down the hall. Those three would likely benefit from getting in touch with their feelings, but Miguel would blossom if he were a part of her after school art therapy program.

"I don't understand how we got stuck buying female supplies."

Mateo Matthews watched as his brother tossed a box of feminine products into the shopping cart. The cardboard box of supplies for a woman's time of the month landed with a dull splat at the bottom of the cart. Mateo lifted the box with a smiling woman on it who definitely did not look as though she was suffering from a feminine ailment and placed it back on the shelf. "That's not the right one."

"Oh, you're an expert in feminine hygiene now?" asked Aldo.

"No, I just know how to read instructions, and

Savy specifically wrote down a different name brand."

Replacing the purple box, Mateo grabbed the pink brand that his sister-in-law had shown him a picture of from the shelf and placed it in the cart. With that last item on their shopping list checked off, they were done with the shopping excursion in town. They'd been back home for less than a week, and it was busier than usual on the ranch with all the Matthews boys home at once, four of their significant others, and a house full of foster kids.

With the rest of the adults having their hands full with ranch chores, repairs, and the general chaos that came with caring for foster kids, Mateo had offered to run errands in town for Savy. He hadn't expected his brother to come along on the domestic mission. But just like when they were kids, Aldo still suffered a bit from separation anxiety.

"The way you act sometimes, *hermano,* you'd think these were for you."

Mateo didn't think for a second that listening to the needs of another person meant that he was somehow feminine. In fact, he didn't think there was anything wrong with the act of listening or with femininity.

"You need to knock it off," said Aldo. "It's ruining my rep."

"You do know that just because we're twins, it doesn't mean we share the same reputation."

Aldo scoffed at that.

Inwardly, Mateo scoffed, too.

For much of their lives, everyone around them had linked the two with the other's behavior because of the way they looked. As identical twins, they looked exactly alike. Though their foster brothers and adoptive parents could always tell them apart, to others, there was no distinction. So Mateo got blamed for a lot of the antics Aldo got up to, whether he agreed with what his brother did or not.

A lot of times, he did not agree.

Especially not the times when Aldo's mean streak made an appearance. Mateo was the lover where Aldo was the fighter. Not so much a fist fighter as a loudmouth.

Aldo had grown up a bully. Not because their biological parents had mistreated their kids. Their parents had wanted nothing but the best for their boys. They just hadn't been able to give it to them, and instead had lost everything when they'd tried.

The social workers and school counselors all

said Aldo's bullying was all about self-sabotaging. He didn't trust that he could have anything good, so he tried to destroy any potential blessings before they could be taken away from him.

Mateo never had anything bad to say about anyone or anything. But because he looked like his brother, people didn't make the distinction between the two, especially not since Mateo often held his tongue and stood by when his brother went off at the mouth.

But for the first time in their lives, the Matthews twins' paths were about to diverge. Mateo was staying home after this last deployment, where Aldo planned to go back into the service. While they were apart, Mateo hoped to settle down, build his own reputation apart from his twin, and perhaps even start to date. He wouldn't admit to his brother that he had one hometown girl in mind: a certain redhead with kind eyes and freckles dotting her cheeks. Green eyes like a dense forest that Mateo got lost in when he daydreamed. And smiling pink lips that made him think of the heart-shaped hard candies he'd once left at her desk on Valentine's Day.

"Hey, look, it's Raggedy Ann."

Mateo frowned. He didn't see a red-haired doll

with yarn for hair and a button nose anywhere in the shop. Belatedly, he remembered that that was the mean nickname his brother had given to the exact girl Mateo had just been daydreaming of. Then, looking up, he caught sight of that beauty.

Kailyn Jade stood in the produce section of the grocery store. There was a shopping basket on one arm, and she held a carrot in her hand. Her gaze was wide, like a deer in headlights, as she stared up at Mateo.

Just like when he was young, Mateo ached to go up to her. To reach out and offer his hand in friendship. To tell her a funny joke, to see her grin go wide and those freckles spread. To give her a heart-shaped candy that said *Be Mine* on it.

But just like when they were young, Kailyn's cheeks went red when she was in his presence, making those freckles disappear in the blush. Those green eyes that he wanted to keep focused on him dropped to the ground. And her slender shoulders hunched forward, like she'd been dealt a blow.

"And look," Aldo continued, "there's Andy."

"Oh, would you look at that," said a carbon copy of Kailyn, but with bone-straight red hair devoid of curls and a pair of glasses set low on her nose. "It's a walking, talking feminine product. Too bad it won't fit down the toilet for a flush. It needs to be taken out with the garbage."

The malicious grin dropped from Aldo's face, and he looked ready for war. Facing off against him, Elayne Jade looked ready to deal the first strike in a battle that had been started years ago but ended in a bitter stalemate.

Mateo opened his mouth, ready at last to defuse this decades-long feud between two of the town's sets of twins. But it was Kailyn's soft voice that broke through the tension.

"We have somewhere to be, Elayne." Kailyn glanced at Mateo and his closed mouth before turning away from him with a dismissive shake of her head. "They're not worth it."

And with that, the Jade twins walked away from the Matthews twins. Mateo was left standing beside his brother, looking for all the world like a solitary *they* when he just wanted to be a *me*. It looked like his dream of asking Kailyn Jade to be a *we* with him would never come true.

CHAPTER FIVE

Unbelievable. A little kid had stood up for another kid that wasn't even his blood in the same halls that this grown man used to haunt. But today, all these years later, the adult-sized Mateo Matthews still couldn't—still wouldn't—stand up to his brother.

When Kailyn had initially spotted him, and their gazes had connected for the first time in years, her traitorous heart had gone skipping down the grocery store aisle. Her feet had nearly followed suit. The way his hazel eyes had gone wide with what looked like delight, the way his nostrils had flared with what might have been desire, the way his lips had quirked in what had seemed a welcoming smile had given her the crazy idea that she could run into his arms and he'd catch her right out of thin air.

The first sight of Mateo Matthews standing in the feminine aisle had been a shock to her senses. He'd grown. He'd grown a lot. He'd filled out in places where she didn't think his body had more space to grow. But it did, and it had grown spectacularly.

He had the kind of chest that was made for a woman to curl up against. His strong arms where he'd looped a basket of feminine products over his left biceps looked like it'd be the perfect thing to lean on during that time of the month. Kailyn envied his girlfriend for having a man that had no issues buying intimate products for her. Except for the fact that he still allowed his brother to bully women.

Because then Aldo had opened his mouth. And Mateo hadn't.

Frog-marching her sister away from Aldo Matthews was Kailyn's number one priority. Now that she was closer to getting funding for her after school art therapy program, she had even less desire to witness Armageddon. She and her sister could hop in their car and go shopping in the next town over if it meant avoiding the Matthews twins and world destruction.

"Why do you always stop me from fighting with that cretin?" said Elayne.

"Why do you always let him get to you?" demanded Kailyn. "You know, name-calling never does any good."

The automatic doors of the grocery store closed behind them. Since they were still standing on the welcome mat, the doors swung back open. Kailyn gave Elayne another tug until they were no longer setting off the sensor, and the doors remained closed.

Elayne opened and closed her fists as she visibly began to calm down. There was still red in her cheeks, and her eyes flashed back to the closed doors of the grocery store. "I don't know why he gets to me like that. I've had people say far worse, but when it comes out of his mouth, I just..."

She turned with a huff to face the other direction. Elayne's hands went on her hips. She even stomped her foot. She reminded Kailyn of the dance a stallion and mare engaged in when they were deciding whether or not to mate.

Kailyn knew that mating with Aldo Matthews was the last thing on her sister's mind. The better

M word would be mar, or better yet, murder. She didn't remember Aldo dating much back in their high school days, though plenty of girls were interested. The only girl who he appeared to pay any attention to was Elayne, and that attention was always negative.

Yeah, the origin of the feud between those two was a mystery—a mystery the whole world wanted unsolved and just buried to never be discovered again.

"Kailyn?"

Kailyn didn't need to turn to know it was Mateo Matthews speaking to her. The softness in his deep voice was in opposition to the hard body she'd witnessed standing in the feminine aisle. She didn't want to turn around, but she didn't have a choice. It was as though magnets pulled her to face him.

Mateo wasn't smiling that almost smile he'd always had reserved for her when they caught each other in the halls or about town without their siblings tagging along. His brows were drawn, not wide with delight at seeing her. His shoulders slumped as though facing her now was a burden. He looked just as stressed by the encounter as she felt.

In his hands, he held a paper bag. A peak over the top of the bag's opening showed that it contained the items that had been in Kailyn's cart before she'd abandoned them to stop World War III. On top sat a pastry bag, food dye, icing, and sprinkles for pastry design.

As the art teacher, Kailyn got a small budget to pay for classroom supplies each year. Those monies were always gone before the first day of school began. After that, Kailyn, like most teachers, came out of pocket to pay for the things necessary for her students' education.

"I didn't pay for those," she said.

"I did."

Mateo held the handle of the paper bag out to her. Instinct and manners had Kailyn reaching for it. Just before the exchange, their fingers touched. The sparks shooting between the two of them made her gasp.

Instinct fired again, warning her to snatch her hand away lest she get burned. She ignored the impulse. Because Mateo's heat felt so good.

His nostrils flared. His throat worked. But once again, Mateo said nothing as a battle waged between them. It was that silence that snapped her out of her stupor and caused her to snatch the bag from his grasp.

"What do I owe you?" she asked.

"I owe you an apology for my brother's behavior."

A profound sense of relief washed over Kailyn's shoulders. These were the words she had been waiting years to hear from this man. She lifted her free hand toward him.

Mateo watched that hand as it rose. They both did. Kailyn had no clue what the hand was planning to do once it reached its destination. She wasn't entirely sure of its destination.

Was her hand planning to pat him on the shoulder in a *there-there* motion?

Perhaps her hand meant to reach out to shake his, to solidify this truce between them.

Or maybe her hand had the crazy idea to smooth the worry creasing his brow, then slide down to cup that strong chin of his.

In the end, the motion and the moment were snatched away as the automatic doors opened again to let loose the raging bull that was Aldo.

"I didn't do anything wrong." Aldo's voice boomed into the cool air, turning it humid.

"Of course that's what he thinks," hissed Elayne.

"Aldo!" Mateo's voice boomed.

"Elayne!" Kailyn's voice joined his.

"Car," they both commanded their siblings.

The power of their voices combined must have worked. Both Aldo and Elayne came to a stunned stop. In unison, they both picked up their feet, marching left-right-left, storming off to their respective cars. When Kailyn turned back to Mateo, he was staring at her.

Slowly, the stress seeped from his face to be replaced by a thoughtful look. His gaze roamed over her. She held still for his perusal, her heart in her throat.

"I'm sorry," he said.

That apology was heavy. It weighed too much to just mean this moment.

"I want there to be peace between us," Mateo continued. "I'm home to stay. We're going to be neighbors and... I'd like... I'd like for us to be friends."

He reached his hand out to her. His didn't pat her on the shoulder. Nor did it reach up to straighten the crease of her brow. His hand aimed at her torso, the exact height for a handshake.

Disappointment coursed through Kailyn. She shook it off and let her manners take over. When

Kailyn reached out to meet his fingers, sparks fluttered across her palm, up her wrists, and settled in the crook of her elbows.

Meeting his eyes, she saw that she wasn't the only one affected. Mateo's Adam's apple bobbed as he regarded her. His eyes were bright again, a mixture of delight and desire. This was not a friendly handshake. It felt like the start of more.

Kailyn's heart beat wildly. Sometimes skipping beats. Sometimes beating twice. With her thumb on Mateo's pulse, she felt the same erratic rhythm coming from him. She was thrilled to know that she wasn't alone in this.

"You two have met. That's good."

For the second time today, Kailyn cringed at the sound of a man's voice who she dreaded interacting with. Aldo huffed inside the passenger seat of a car off in the distance. On the other side of the parking lot, Elayne sat in the driver's seat of her car, glaring up at the sky. Coming up to Kailyn and Mateo at the store front was Owen.

"I guess this handshake means you two are working it out." Owen stepped between Mateo and Kailyn's clasped hands, causing them to break apart. Stepping around Kailyn, much like a dog eying a fire hydrant, he placed an arm around Kailyn's shoulders.

Mateo's warm gaze darkened.

Kailyn stepped away from Owen's unwanted embrace. "What do you mean? Working what out?"

"Captain Matthews is in line for the after school funding, too."

CHAPTER SIX

ateo could only concentrate on the hand around Kailyn's waist. His fingers clenched into fists, mostly to keep from reaching out and wrenching the guy away from her. But once they were in fists, he realized that he could do more damage. Taking a deep breath, he forced his hands to relax.

He relaxed even more when Kailyn stepped away from the man, as though his touch offended her. The interloper made to move closer, to regain his hold on her. Mateo clenched his hands into fists again, prepared to disabuse him of the notion.

He wouldn't need to. Kailyn took another step away from the guy. Her step brought her between the two of them. Mateo got the clear notion that she wasn't interested in breaking up any possible fight between the two unevenly matched males. Her attention wasn't even on the other guy. It rested solely on him.

"You're my competition for the after school funding?" she asked, pointing an accusing finger at him.

There were specks of paint on that finger. She must have been painting recently. He wanted to know what she'd created. Kailyn appeared to want an answer to his question because she spoke up again, her finger jabbing at him once more.

"Let me guess; you want to create some sort of military program? Like an RTOC?"

"JROTC," Mateo corrected. "Junior Reserve Officers' Training Corps."

Kailyn's eyes were bright with—what was that? Betrayal? Shock? Disbelief? Whatever it was, his fingers now ached to smooth furrowed line between her brows. Maybe not with his hands. It would be best to do those with his lips.

"You want to make child soldiers?"

That was disgust in her voice. He knew that tone too well. It sounded exactly like her sister's voice whenever Elayne engaged Aldo.

"Officers," Mateo said.

"Officers who fight in wars as soldiers."

"The program teaches kids to become leaders and managers. It could even pay for their college career."

Kailyn huffed, crossing her arms over her chest. She looked away from him, toward the other guy. The other guy smirked at Mateo, but when he made a move to swoop his tentacles around Kailyn again, she moved away. The fact that she had no desire to be touched by this man pleased Mateo to no end. But he still couldn't wrap his head around why she was so angry.

"You want to start an after school art program?" he asked.

Mateo was surprised there wasn't already one. He knew Kailyn was the art teacher at the high school. He'd kept tabs on her, casually bringing up her name whenever he'd call to chat with one of the James or Silver sisters. Between the nine of them, they knew everything and everyone in Honor Valley.

Having the JROTC program run through the school had been Mateo's first step in getting closer to Kailyn. He figured if they were colleagues, it would be easier to bump into her and strike up a conversation, a friendship, a relationship.

Had Mateo known that she was angling to teach art after school, he would've been the first in line to take her class. He remembered watching her paint in the high school art studio when he was supposed to be doing drills on the football fields. She always looked so peaceful as she swiped the brush across the canvas. He'd always sneak in afterwards to see what she'd created. He wasn't much for art or interpretation, but looking at her paintings always made something warm bloom in his chest.

"Of course I want to teach kids art." Kailyn took another step away from the man who stupidly still had his arm outstretched to her, though it was clear she'd forgotten he was even there.

Kailyn stepped up toe to toe with Mateo. That finger still hung between them. If he leaned forward, Mateo was the one in danger of being knocked out. A simple touch from her would've floored him. His knees shook when he inhaled Kailyn's fresh floral scent. There was a hint of paint chemicals coming off her pale skin.

"Art therapy has the capacity to heal so many children's inner wounds," she went on. "It allows children, and adults, to express themselves without having to verbalize past traumas and hurts."

Mateo liked the sound of that. He especially liked the idea of healing under this woman's capable hands and caring guidance. Her index finger had stopped pointing. The other four fingers of her hands came to stand by that lone soldier. For a moment, Mateo thought she'd touch his heart.

"I want to teach them how to manage their feelings." Kailyn balled her open hand into a fist and placed it over her chest. "You want to teach them how to shut them down and hurt someone else?"

"No," Mateo said softly. "I want to show them how to fight for what they believe in."

"Why do they have to fight at all? Isn't fighting and violence and strife the cause of all problems?"

"No," he said again, his voice remaining soft. "Art and combat are different sides of the same coin. One is used to protect the other. The other gives you something to fight for."

There was confusion on her brow, but it outweighed the anger and indignation.

"I don't see why we can't have both," Mateo continued. "We could run both programs together."

Kailyn's lips parted. She chewed at her lower lip, unsure. Mateo reached for her, and that's when the other guy stepped back into the scene.

"There's only enough funding for one program." His hand went around her waist again. "As vice principal and the administrator in charge of recreational programs for the high school, you have my full support, Kailyn."

Kailyn flinched at his touch, but she didn't pull away this time. Her lips remained pursed as she regarded Mateo. Unfortunately, she didn't have any more words for him.

Mateo knew the funding was as good as his. The vice principal might be in charge of the recreational program for the school, but he couldn't grant the funding. If he could, he would've already handed it over to Kailyn—and Mateo wouldn't blame him. He would've done the same. But right now, it was the VP who had his hands on the thing Mateo wanted most in this world. His fighting instincts wanted to kick in. But he knew that wouldn't work with a gentle soul like Kailyn.

She hated fighting. She craved peace. But Mateo knew that he was right; art and combat were often two sides of the same coin. He would simply have to fight to get her to see the other side.

CHAPTER SEVEN

ailyn rubbed at her eyes. Her hands came away wet. Not wet from tears. It was a thicker wetness, with a good deal of viscosity. Looking down at the red streak on her palm, she knew she had smeared paint across her forehead.

It wouldn't be the first time. At least she'd caught it. Not that anyone was around to see.

It was the end of a long school day. The end of an even longer week. On Monday, she had assigned self-portraits in many of her art classes. She'd given students the leeway to use any materials they saw fit. Self-portraits were more of a window into a person's soul than the eyes were.

Because the portrait didn't show what was in the mirror, it showed what was in their mind's eye.

Kailyn sighed as she flipped through the turned-in presentations. Kameron Harris, the quarterback and homecoming king, had drawn a football in green grass with a crown. He was finished on the first day of the assignment and spent the rest of the class chatting with the other jocks at his table thinking he'd gotten over and had gotten an easy A. Little did he know that Kailyn saw the clear cry for help in his portrait. The kid thought that this was all he could ever be, but he clearly yearned for more. If not, then why would he have painstakingly drawn each blade of grass getting greener the further away from the football the blades got?

Mika Devin, who was the uncontested fron-trunner for class valedictorian, drew herself with full regalia befitting that honor. Also around her neck was a stethoscope. Instead of the royal blue and regal purple school colors, she wore a white lab coat. Aside from blue eyes, there was no other facial feature on her drawing. And unlike Kameron's creation, the rest of her canvas was blank. The poor girl was clearly under so much pressure.

The rest of the portraits were much the same. Black and white portraits that spoke loudly of depression. Neon-colored paintings that made Kailyn wonder about oversensitivity. The kids were all crying out for help. The question was, would any of them take the solution Kailyn wanted to offer?

Kailyn set the children's canvases aside and turned back to her own. While they had worked on depicting themselves, she had done a different painting exercise, one where she let the brush do what it wanted. Kind of a stream of consciousness painting. What her rational mind saw emerging from the canvas was a certain tall, dark, and handsome soldier.

She had never drawn him before. Not exactly. His eyes had a appeared a few times in drawings. That small smile that had always felt so big to her was reflected in more paintings than she cared to admit. But she'd never drawn a full-figured depiction of Mateo Matthews before.

And she'd drawn the warmonger in a pastoral scene, no less. Daisies and tulips dotted the green background, while he stood tall and proud in— were those fatigues? Yes, she'd drawn him in fatigues, though she wasn't even sure if a pilot wore fatigues.

It didn't matter. He was the enemy. He'd allowed his brother to be mean to her sister without any interference. And now he wanted to turn troubled youths into violent aggressors.

Kailyn jabbed at the canvas. The angry brush strokes ruined her pastoral scene. They muted the fatigues. But not a single bristle so much as smudged his smile.

"Wow, that's cool. It's like two opposing artists working on the same painting."

Kailyn dropped the paintbrush as though it was a cookie stolen from the treats jar. The paint splattered on the floor, leaving behind a starburst pattern. Instead of facing her sister, she grabbed a wad of paper towels and dabbed at the mess.

"He looks familiar, but I can't place him. Who is he?"

"He's no one," Kailyn stammered as she straightened. "I was just messing around."

"Whoever he is, he's beautiful."

Kailyn wanted to chuck the brush and the canvas against the wall. The angry art couldn't be beautiful. But looking at it, she could see the appeal in the softness beneath the harsh strokes.

Maybe she should tell her sister who her unconscious inspiration was? That would certainly get Elayne to stop admiring the piece.

"You, on the other hand, need a bit of prettying up." Elayne grabbed a rag and came at Kailyn.

Kailyn made a half-hearted dodge away from her sister. Older by twenty minutes, Elayne liked to play mom to her from time to time. Every single time she did, Kailyn ate it up.

Neither of them could remember receiving this kind of attention from their birth mother. From what they'd been told, she had been a teenager herself. She'd kept the girls for a few months, but without any support from her own parents or their birth father, who was not named on the birth certificate, she'd turned the twins over to the state. She died in a factory accident a few years later.

"Better?" asked Kailyn after her sister had caught and cleaned her face of any remaining streaks of paint.

"Eh, you'll do." Elayne tossed the rag in the sink. "Listen, I wanted to say I'm sorry."

"About what?"

"About yesterday with the Matthews. I'm a grown woman. I'm a counselor to kids. I need to stop letting Aldo Matthews get to me like that. Next time I see him, I'm going to be cordial."

"I'll believe that when I see it."

Elayne cut her a look.

Kailyn held up her hands in mock defense. "I mean, I would like to see that."

And she really would. She did want to see a truce between Elayne and Aldo. But there would be no easy truce between her and Mateo. Not while he stood in the way of her plans.

Kailyn opted not to tell that to Elayne. There was war, and then there was intergalactic destruction. If Elayne knew that any of the Matthews were going against her baby sister, she'd go nuclear. Best if Kailyn handled this battle herself.

She could beat Mateo Matthews. Her presentation skills would be top-notch. What Elayne had already added to the slides yesterday couldn't be beat. And she did have Owen's support. She had this in the bag.

"Well, I'm off," said Elayne. "Just wanted to say that and goodbye before I head out for my trip."

"I hope you enjoy your conference."

"Excuse me, Ms. Jade."

The little chef from yesterday, Miguel, stood in the doorway. Seeing that the visitor was for

Kailyn, Elayne waved goodbye and stepped through the door.

"Hi, Miguel," said Kailyn, beckoning the kid inside.

"You said you had some decorating tools I could borrow?"

She did. They were the ones she'd gone to the grocery store for the other day. The ones she'd nearly left in the middle of the aisle to get her sister away from her nemesis. The same appliances that Mateo Matthews had purchased and given to her as a peace offering. Well, at least now they'd be put to good use.

"You're welcome to keep them," Kailyn said, handing over the bag of goods.

Miguel's eyes lit up.

"Hurry now. I don't want you to miss the after school bus."

"Someone from my family is coming to pick me up."

Oh? She'd thought the boy was a foster after that confrontation the other day? Maybe he was being raised by relatives?

"I'm going to be adopted," Miguel said proudly. "They start the paperwork this week. That's why I want to make a special dessert."

"Congratulations, Miguel. I was a foster kid and then adopted, too."

"I didn't know that," he said, sitting down in one of the plastic chairs. "Was it a big family?"

"No, just my mom and dad and my sister."

"I'm getting two sisters, three brothers, and a whole bunch of aunts and uncles. I'm even getting a grandpa."

"That sounds amazing."

"It's great. I didn't think I'd like my uncles. They're all soldiers, and I thought they would make me run drills or shoot guns."

"Soldiers?"

"Yup. But Uncle Will said a soldier's first weapon is his mind, not his gun. Uncle Topher said he'd take his girlfriend's mind over any of theirs. And then Aunt Foxy said Ms. Toni—that's Uncle Topher's girlfriend—wouldn't be his girlfriend for long. She's clairscent—clairscenty—clairsentient. Aunt Foxy is, not Ms. Toni. Do you know what that means?"

Kailyn did know what that meant. She knew most of those people and their names. They were kids who had been at the Bright Horizon's Foster Home when she and her sister had been there. The boys had been adopted by the Matthews couple.

The James girls had gone with their mother for a time before the eldest, Savy, had come of age and was able to claim responsibility for her two sisters.

"I'm making a celebratory cake, and it's going to have my new name on it; Miguel Matthews."

Kailyn tried to smile for the boy, but her lips wouldn't stretch.

"Oh, there's my ride now."

Kailyn looked up to see Mateo Matthews standing in the door. She was transported back almost a decade ago when he'd leaned over the water fountain or gone around a corner headed to football practice, or catch her eye in the cafeteria. There was that small smile he gave her that set off something big inside of her. Like it always did, her heart skipped a beat at the sight of him, and the air rushed from her lungs with a longing sigh.

CHAPTER EIGHT

Walking down the halls of his alma mater didn't bring up strong emotions for Mateo. High school hadn't been a dark place for him like some students. He'd had his share of popularity, though he had never let it go to his head. With his athletic build, he had always been a first pick by all the sports coaches for any team he tried out for. Since his parents demanded the effort, his grades were up to par, though not exactly Principal's Honor Roll. Because girls seemed to find manners charming, he was never without attention. Still, he'd only ever cared about having one girl's attentions.

Each day in this place had been broken into BK and AK. Before he saw Kailyn Jade in the halls and after he saw her. Her grades were better than his, so he hadn't been in any of her classes. He'd only ever catch glimpses of her in the halls. Oftentimes he'd go out of his way to make sure their paths would cross.

In tenth grade, they'd shared a lunch period. She'd sat with her sister, which made his approach tricky. He'd been steadily maneuvering his friend group's seating closer and closer to the table she sat with her sister and friends each day. Unfortunately, a few weeks into the semester, Aldo had managed to get switched to his lunch period, and the lunchroom had been divided into a war zone he could never safely navigate across.

In eleventh grade, his third period math class was right next door to hers. After a few days, he'd noted that she always lingered behind to talk with the teacher. Math, apparently, wasn't her best subject, and she never left without asking for clarifications on the day's lessons. Mateo developed the habit of lingering behind, too. He'd almost timed it right when Aldo started popping up at the end of the hall to hurry him along to the next class, which they shared.

By twelfth grade, he was out of ideas. Not about crossing Kailyn's path, about keeping his brother off his trail. But Mateo did have one failsafe.

The one place he would always see the object of his affection was the art room. Before school, after school, and sometimes during the lunch period. He knew every route that would lead him past the art room, and he braved many late passes to go that way.

Nearly a decade later, Mateo still knew the way by heart. Instead of waiting for Miguel in the pickup line, he made his way into the building. Got a visitor's pass. Then made his way down the winding hall.

When he came up to the door, his teenage heart pounded at the front of his chest, just like it had every time he'd catch a glimpse of her eight years ago. Kailyn stood in front of the windows, the sunlight streaming in to curl around her strawberry-colored hair.

"Kailyn."

Mateo didn't so much as say her name as he breathed it. It was both the prayer and the answer. It was both a plea and an expression of gratitude.

All the years he'd been gone fell away. All of the strife between their siblings evaporated as they stood gazing at one another. She was surrounded by color, and he felt like he'd been walking around in a monotone world.

There would be no more Aldo to block his path. There would be no more staying quiet in the face of any fights or arguments that didn't involve the two of them. Mateo was done with it. He was done holding his tongue and redirecting his steps to the one thing he'd ever wanted all to himself.

Mateo wasn't waiting any longer for the life he wanted to begin. He took a step across the threshold of the art room. Each step brought him closer and closer to where he had always dreamed of being.

When he reached her, Mateo's instinct was to wrap his arms around Kailyn and pull her to him. Because finally he could. There was nothing to stop him. Nothing except the single finger she held between them—that same finger she'd held up yesterday when she'd learned that he was her competition for the after-school program funding.

"What are you doing here?" she asked.

There was no bite to her words, only a breathless quality. It sounded close to surrender. With her finger as her only weapon, she was otherwise defenseless. As deterrents went, that single digit wasn't much. Her fingers were weapons he wanted to gently dismantle one by one with a kiss to each of her finger pads.

"I knew you'd be here." He spoke the truth he'd wanted to say the four years they'd inhabited these halls together.

"Me?" she asked.

"He means me, Ms. Jade."

Both Kailyn and Mateo frowned at the voice that came from the side. From the corner of his eyes, Mateo saw Miguel standing there watching the two of them. Miguel wasn't watching them closely in the way that Denny or LaTisha would. Those two kids would've immediately seen what was between Mateo and Kailyn. Miguel was still at that stage of adolescence where he didn't notice, or simply wasn't interested, in the attraction between men and women.

Miguel held up a bag. Mateo belatedly recognized it as the bag of groceries and appliances he'd purchased for Kailyn the other day.

"I got what I needed," said Miguel. "Now we can go home so I can decorate my cake."

"You bought those for Miguel?" Mateo asked Kailyn.

"You're his foster brother?" Kailyn asked Mateo.

"Foster uncle, I think." Mateo grinned. "Charlie and Savy are adopting him and all the kids that were at Bright Horizons. Didn't you know? The foster house got moved onto my family's ranch."

Kailyn shook her head, but she smiled as she did so. And wonder of wonders, that finger lowered. She was no longer on the attack.

"I had heard the home was moving," she said. "That's good. That's great."

Her smile spread. First while she was looking at Miguel. Then it spread to Mateo.

Mateo took the opportunity to move in closer. He wasn't cornering her, per se. She wasn't his enemy. But he had no intention of letting his target get away. "You should invite Ms. Jade to your celebration dinner, Miguel."

Kailyn's green gaze flared at the suggestion. She took a step back. Too late, she realized she had nowhere to go. "You don't have to—"

"Please come," said Miguel. "I'm still having trouble with pairing the right colors."

Kailyn swallowed. Her gaze went first to the intent warrior towering over her whom she couldn't possibly hope to get around. Then at the child, who gazed up at her with pleading, innocent eyes. She was well and truly cornered and trapped.

She took a deep breath and nodded. It wasn't a white flag, but it was a laying down of arms. A surrender.

Mateo had won this battle. He would be ruthless to win every battle he could until the war between them was over. Until he showed this woman that there was a lifetime of peace to be found in his arms.

CHAPTER NINE

The click of the passenger door closing should have felt like the slam of a jail cell. No, not a jail cell. The padded wall of an insane asylum. What normal person would willingly climb into the car of their nemesis and then allow said nemesis to shut them inside? Apparently, that abnormal person was Kailyn.

Because to Kailyn, that quiet snick didn't feel like a trap. It didn't feel like an end. It felt like something that had been wide open for far too long, clicking right into place.

"Seatbelt," said Mateo.

Of her own free will, Kailyn reached for the leather belt and pulled it across her middle, effectively strapping herself in. There was a phenomenon when a hostage stopped fighting their captor and began welcoming their captivity. Stockholm syndrome, it was called.

That had to be what she was experiencing as she sat calmly in the passenger seat as Mateo Matthews drove her away from the high school. She caught a brief sight of Owen thumbing the fob to his sports car. He frowned in their direction. It was that kind of look where you think you might know someone, but you didn't get a close enough look to be sure.

Kailyn was sure Owen hadn't placed her. The light of recognition didn't brighten his gaze. More importantly, that misplaced look of possession never crossed his features.

When she had climbed into Owen's car on the first date, she had felt something prickle at the back of her neck. Not danger. Just a feeling that she was in the wrong place with the wrong person.

The sensations running across her skin right now weren't prickles. They were tingles. Kailyn felt the fine hairs on her body stand at attention. Not out of fear. There was a sense of excitement that urged her to sit forward, to lean toward Mateo and his heat.

Kailyn kept her back pressed firmly into the

passenger seat. She folded her hands in her lap, twining her fingers together until they were on lockdown. She pressed her lips together so that no words could escape and concentrated on making her breaths deep and steady.

Neither of the adults in the car said much on the drive. There wasn't much silence to fill in. Miguel kept up a steady stream of conversation about the ingredients he was going to use in his cake. Once those details were outlined, he started in on the makings of the icing.

Mateo smiled indulgently at the kid from the rearview mirror. He'd *hmm* and *ahh* at the appropriate intervals to show he was paying attention, but Kailyn knew Mateo wasn't engaged in Miguel's recipe. Just as much as she wasn't invested in his choice of food coloring combinations for the icing.

She was focused on how little space there was on the middle console where Mateo rested his right hand. Her fingers dangled over the arm rest so close to his. A bump in the road or a pothole and they'd be holding hands. She should remind him that the proper position for road driving was hands at ten and two.

Kailyn kept her lips sealed. There was too much danger of something else entirely escaping her mouth about what Mateo Matthews could do with his hands.

The scent of his cologne was like one of those visible cartoon clouds. It was doing something funny to her brain. Maybe he was drugging her? Because all she could think was how much she wanted to lean over, bury her nose in his neck, and take a good strong whiff.

Those rumbling assents Mateo gave to Miguel had her crossing her legs toward him. Only to uncross and turn away from him. Which would then expose the back of her neck to him. Those *hmms* and *ahhs* then tickled the space behind her ear, causing her to shudder and then turn back toward him.

Not to mention that her heart was skipping every other beat now that he was a constant in her presence. Before, she'd only had glimpses of him in the hall. She'd been in his presence for a half an hour at this point, and she wasn't sure her body, her entire being, could take much more.

Finally, the torture was over. They turned off the main streets of the town and began down a long drive. To the left was the Silver Star Ranch, a place Kailyn had been a couple of times over the years. She'd been casual friends with Tilly and

Gunny, the Silver twins. Those two had gotten married recently, and both Kailyn and Elayne had been invited to their weddings. Mateo had still been in his last deployment at that time.

Instead of turning left, they turned right. It was a direction Kailyn had never taken in this town. In the space of a breath, the sprawling lands of the Flying Cross Ranch came into view.

The scene looked like it had been painted by Van Gogh. The shades of blue sky meeting and mingling with the gradations of green pasture were simply breathtaking. The landscape looked unreal, yet so detailed that she had the thought that if she reached out, she could smear the vivid paint.

The passenger car door opened, and another work of art stepped into her view. Mateo looked like he'd walked off the canvas. A flawless creation from the Crayola Colors of the World collection. When he reached out his Medium Almond colored palm to her, Kailyn placed her Light Rose fingers in his, eager to be pulled into the mural.

"Charlie and Savy spruced up the bunkhouse where we used to sleep," Mateo said, pointing to what looked like an overlarge, long and narrow barn. "And they're adding prefab houses for my brothers and their wives. The Silver sisters are helping with that project. Other than that, it hasn't changed much since we were kids."

"I've never been here before," said Kailyn.

The reason why she had never been to his home before was left unspoken.

"Aldo's out of town for a couple of days," he said.

"So's Elayne."

The air around them changed. It had been heavy with things left unsaid. It lightened considerably under the absence of their siblings.

A cool breeze blew between them as Miguel shot past them and into the house. A little blonde girl eyed them curiously from the porch. There was a broom in her hand as she swept the wood slats. Below the porch, a brown-skinned girl was down on her knees as she dug her hands into the rich earth. Off to the side, Kailyn saw two other young boys fussing over a bale of hay. Both boys were pale skin with fair hair. One had his hair done in silky cornrows. The other boy Kailyn recognized as Denny.

"It looks like you're running a child labor farm," she said.

"You're just determined to think the worst of us, aren't you?" said Mateo.

There was no bite to his words. Just patience. Along with a vulnerability. His hand twitched. She half expected him to let her go, but his hold didn't loosen. Instead, he jerked his head in the direction of the children, indicating that she should follow.

"This is a working ranch, so everyone pulls their weight. Kids sleep in during school year, but they have chores after school and on the weekend."

"You could hire ranch hands."

"Or we could use this to teach them responsibility, how to care for the land and the animals. Equally, it's a lesson in how families work together and take pride in their home."

Looking closer at the kids, she saw that they weren't frowning or angry. They were a bit sweaty. But the occasional laugh sounded, along with good-natured joking. The two boys with the hay weren't alone. The tall figure of Charlie Matthews came up behind them and patted them both on the back.

"Kailyn Jade, is that you?"

Savy James squinted at her from the open door of the house. Her eyes went wide with recognition, and she let the porch door slam behind her as she came toward Kailyn, arms outstretched.

"I'm covered in paint," said Kailyn.

"I'm covered in ranch," said Savy. "Girl, get in here."

Even when they were both scared foster kids, Savy had always given the best hugs. Her hugs and her singing voice were the only thing Kailyn missed about being in the Bright Horizon's Foster Home.

"You don't seem surprised to see me here," said Kailyn.

"Why would I? Mateo's had a crush on you since we were all in foster care."

"He has not."

Behind her, Mateo said nothing. He didn't look embarrassed. He didn't deny it either. He just held her gaze. Kailyn's palms warmed from where he had held her hand only seconds ago. It felt like they were still connected.

"And Aldo's always had a thing for Elayne."

That brought an expression and a grunt of dissent from Mateo. Kailyn echoed both his loud facial expression as well as his vocal protest.

"They can't stand each other," said Kailyn.

Savy shrugged. "Boys tug the pigtails of girls they like until they know how to behave better."

Just then, Charlie came up and tugged at one of his wife's wayward curls. She swatted at him good-naturedly before turning back to Kailyn. Charlie Matthews had never tugged at Savy's pigtails when they were kids. He'd professed his feelings for her clearly. Aldo had gone in on Elayne from day one, clearly stating his dislike. Whereas Mateo had said nothing.

Savy was right about her particular Matthews. But Kailyn wasn't so sure her insight was clear on the other two Matthews boys.

CHAPTER TEN

"Miguel, you outdid yourself. We are the luckiest family in the world to be getting a son like you."

Miguel's eyes sparkled under Savy's praise. Around the table, heads nodded in assent. Well, the adult heads all did. The pride and love in Savy's and Charlie's eyes was brighter than the overhead dining room light. Foxy winked at Miguel, and her husband, Joe, gave the kid a thumbs-up. At the head of the table, Father Matthews rubbed at his belly as a satisfied grin stretched across his brown face.

Denny, the tallest kid, rolled his eyes, but he couldn't hide the small uptilt of his lips as he took another bite of the dessert Miguel had prepared.

The two girls grinned broadly, and the third boy with blond braids in his hair nodded his head once.

While he'd been away, Mateo's family had grown. But in so many ways, it had remained the same.

Just as it was when he'd first sat down at this table as a scared and confused adolescent. He looked up to see that he wasn't alone. He was sitting with a family. A real tight-knit family. With rules and rituals and discipline and deep affection. The Matthews homestead was bursting at the seams at the moment. But Mateo knew they would always make space for more.

Mateo watched Kailyn as she used her dinner napkin to dab first at the corner of her mouth and second at the corner of her eye. When she raised her head, she met his gaze. She lowered her eyes, but only for a second. Looking up at him from beneath her lashes, she offered Mateo a shy grin.

Mateo sat his knife and fork down on his plate. Then he placed his hands below the table. It wasn't enough. He lifted and sat on his hands. He had no other choice. More than anything in this world, he wanted to launch across the table and taste that grin.

But there were rules and rituals in this family. Chief amongst them was no mauling the girl you had been in love with since childhood at the dinner table. That one had come courtesy of Charlie and Savy about a decade or so ago.

Mateo wanted to strip the shyness away from her grin. He wanted Kailyn to open up to him fully, to show him her emotions. He wanted her to know it was okay to be vulnerable in front of him. He wanted to capture each one of the tears that had threatened her eyes and let them know it was safe to fall because he would catch them. He would catch her. He wanted to taste the smiles that came to her lips. He wanted to hold that hand that made the world so much more beautiful.

He wanted her. Always had. Always would.

Looking down at the calluses on his hands from his time in battle, he wondered if she would ever let him. Kailyn was a gentle soul. She had always gravitated toward the beauty in the world. Where the underbelly of society always showed itself to him.

"I didn't know that the foster home had moved to the ranch," Kailyn said.

"It was Charlie's idea," said Savy.

"It was my only option to finally get this

woman to marry me." Charlie planted a kiss atop his wife's head. Savy's hand snaked around to stroke his cheek. A secret smile was on both their faces.

"In some ways these kids brought us all together," said Foxy. "Joe and I finally admitted our feelings when we went to look in on Daria when she was in state custody."

"*You* admitted your feelings." Joe held up a finger. "*I* never made any secret of how I felt about you."

"Ash brought the two of us together," Tricksy said with her gaze on Will.

"I did make a secret of how I felt about her," said Will.

It was a poorly kept secret in this house. All of the Matthews boys had known that Will was head over heels in love with Tricksy. Well, all of them except Topher. But Topher rarely noticed anything outside of a mirror.

"From what I understand, that was your fault." Toni Solis raised an eyebrow at Topher.

For once, Topher wasn't trying to catch a glimpse of himself. His attention was entirely focused on the woman at his side. His arm was casually draped behind her chair, but his fingers kept playing in the braided ends of her hair.

"We all know I don't keep secrets. I told you exactly how I felt…" Topher frowned, looking off into the distance. "As soon as I understood what it was that I felt."

A chorus of laughter went around the table. Mateo had missed this during his time in the service. Sure, he had a family of soldiers in his unit. But nothing could ever replace the years and the scraps and the scars and the love of his family.

"Everyone's married or engaged except the twins," said Savy, her gaze falling not on Mateo, but on Kailyn.

Mateo got the urge to wave frantically in front of Savy. He wanted to make every signal to stop, slow down, and caution that he knew. Not because he didn't want to go down that path. Because he didn't want to scare Kailyn away. But maybe keeping secret how he felt about her was doing him a disservice. It certainly hadn't worked for any of his brothers.

"Oh, that won't be for long," said Foxy as casually as she would announce the weather forecast for the next day. "Aldo's getting married this weekend."

Silence zinged around the table. Foxy fancied herself a psychic—clairsentient, to be exact. But she was only right fifty percent of the time. This would definitely be one of the times she got it wrong. Aldo was off discussing a private military contract job.

"Whether or not the marriage will last, I can't see." Foxy rubbed at her eyelids.

"On that note," said Charlie, "it's time for bed."

There was only a cursory protest from the kids. They'd had a long day at school, followed by chores, and now their bellies were overfull. Even if they didn't think they'd fall asleep soon, they'd be proven wrong pretty quickly. They all got up and marched to the bunkhouse like good little soldiers.

Mateo used the distraction of the kids going off to bed to get Kailyn all to himself. She had had a long day of school herself. Her plate was cleared, and Savy had packed her some leftovers in Tupperware. It was the perfect time for the two of them to escape.

Kailyn said her good nights to everyone with promises not to be a stranger. Father Matthews gave his son a knowing look, which Mateo returned with a sly grin before handing Kailyn into the car. No, this woman was not going to be a stranger for long.

"I always expected you to go into the art field," said Mateo as they turned out of the long drive. "I'm surprised you're not selling your art."

"I do. But I find it more rewarding to use art to help those in pain or distress."

"I've heard about that—art therapy? Some of the soldiers with PTSD did that on base."

Kailyn tilted her head to one side, looking out at the starry sky. "I usually work with kids. I never thought of working with soldiers."

"I think it helped. I think any program where you can get someone to face their issues head-on helps. Especially if it leaves the world a better place. That's why many men and women go into the armed services to begin with: to make the world a better place."

She seemed to think about that, but she didn't offer any commentary. All too soon, he had pulled up to her house. He remembered it from when he was young. He'd heard that her parents had passed away a few years ago.

Like his family, Kailyn and her sister had kept the house mostly the same. It was still painted white, likely a fresh coat sometime in the last five years. The trim was a deep green that he could make out under the streetlights. But the dormers were painted in a colorful array. Those were new. They had to be Kailyn's artistic touches.

Parking on the street, Mateo walked around the car in time to hand her out. Her hand in his was a jolt to his system. It was the third time he'd touched her today. Each time had been at the passenger car door. Mateo had half a mind to ask her to go on a joy ride with him just so that he could hand her in and then out of the car again.

A wind blew, shifting a strand of vibrant red hair into her face. Kailyn brushed the strand away, but one tuft of hair refused to stay out of her eyes. Mateo could't blame it. Without thinking it through, he reached and tugged the hair from her eyes and tucked it behind her ear. When his gaze met hers, she was staring at him.

There was something in her gaze. He'd seen it before. H"d seen it each time he came upon her in the halls. He knew it all too well because it was what he felt when he looked at her during those brief stolen moments. It was hesitancy.

A hesitancy before she decided whether or not to acknowledge his presence. A hesitancy before she confirmed it was safe to smile. A hesitancy before taking a step toward the something more that had always lingered between them before either or both of their siblings burst onto the scene.

Kailyn didn't look quite so hesitant now. Mateo stepped closer. She tilted up her head. Her lips parted. His nostrils flared. Her gaze dipped to his lips. Mateo leaned in, but a call from a man's voice jerked them apart.

CHAPTER ELEVEN

When Mateo Matthews tugged at Kailyn's hair, she knew it wasn't an act of misbehavior. The way the pad of his forefinger lightly brushed her temple before seizing the runaway strands spoke volumes that this was a man in command. The way he wound the tendril of hair around the length of his finger loudly proclaimed that he was a man of strategy. He had her cornered, trapped, and as his captive, her body would go anywhere he directed her to go.

Forget Stockholm syndrome. Kailyn wasn't in some foreign land kidnapped by a twirly mustached villain she didn't know. She was in the familiar surroundings of Honor Valley, walking straight into the well-lit embrace of the man she had always secretly yearned to be near.

With his index finger trapped by her hair, Kailyn's head dipped to brush against the tips of Mateo's three other fingers. His thumb caught her cheek, and his hand opened to welcome the side of her face into the palm of his hand. The heat she'd felt from his fingertips was nothing compared to the full force furnace of his entire hand.

From somewhere deep inside her, a voice shouted *Home.* Something in her chest sighed in that way where, after a long journey in a car, she looked out the window and spotted her street. Mateo Matthews was more than her street. He was the safe place she'd been looking for her whole life.

As a foster kid, Kailyn had been without a home for a relatively short period of time. But the fear and uncertainty in that brief time period had taken root at the back of her mind and made a permanent home. She'd always been the quintessential good girl to her foster parents because, though that feeling never went away, she never wanted it to become her reality again. She never wanted to be without a home of her own again.

Resting in the relatively small space of Mateo's hand, her breathing came easily. The perpetually tight muscles of her back went slack, and her shoulders loosened. There wasn't a single tendon of tension inside her body. She would've equated the feeling to that of nothingness, except she felt everything, everywhere, all at once.

Kailyn got the sense that no matter where she went, or how far she traveled, as long as Mateo was with her, she would never be far from home.

She opened her eyes, having just realized that she had closed them when she'd given her head over to his capable hand, and looked up into his gaze. Kailyn might not have had a lot of experience with men, but she knew desire when she saw it. It was shining brightly in Mateo's dark gaze.

Savy was right. Boys might tug at a girl's hair to get her attention until he knew how to behave better. Mateo was behaving in exactly the way a woman would want.

He was behaving in exactly the way she wanted. There was no friction between them. Everything was easy and peaceful. Kailyn could've stayed just like this for the rest of the night. For the rest of her life.

"There you are."

Owen's voice was like a record scratch on a classical piece of music. It wasn't the first time he'd shown up at her house unannounced. It had been a long time since he'd tried it. Kailyn was sure the only reason he'd tried now was because Elayne was out of town.

"I've been waiting for you to get home." Owen's narrowed gaze was focused on Mateo, not Kailyn. The corners of his mouth and eyes twitched, much in the same way Kailyn's would when she was faced with a particularly daunting math problem that didn't add up.

"Why would you be waiting for me to get home?" Kailyn twinned her fingers with Mateo's. She brought their hands down between them as they both stepped toward the latched gate that led to her front door.

Owen's confusion shifted. It darkened a bit as he glared at Kailyn and Mateo's laced fingers. "Your car was still at school. I was concerned."

"Thank you for your concern, Vice Principal Sharp. But as you can see, I'm perfectly okay."

Mateo's hand had dropped from hers. For a brief second, Kailyn panicked. She slipped into that dark hopelessness she'd felt when she realized that she wasn't like other kids, she didn't have a mom and dad or a home to call her own. That feeling when she realized she didn't have much protection in this world aside from her sister.

She wanted to grab for Mateo. For his hand. For his arms. For any part of him and bring it back around her.

She didn't need to.

Barely a fraction of a second passed before Mateo's free hand came to rest at her low back. Those same fingers that had twined around her hair, that had laced with her own, dug just a little bit into her hip. It was a clear sign of possession, and Kailyn was here for it.

Mateo's possession felt more secure than her adoption papers. More secure than her name on the deed her parents had left her and her sister. Her parents had passed from this world. The house could be blown away by a crazy act of nature, like a tornado or earthquake. But Mateo's hand, that felt like it would never leave her side.

"Why don't I walk you inside?" said Owen, still oblivious to the status of their non-existent, never-had-existed relationship.

Kailyn felt Mateo bristle. She tensed in his hold. The last thing she wanted was a confrontation between these men.

It wasn't that she feared for Mateo's well-being.

No one with eyes would look at these two men and worry for the dark-haired one. With the touch of his pinky finger, Mateo would flatten Owen onto the sidewalk. That show of violence was something Kailyn never wanted to witness. Not from the person she had decided to trust her heart to.

"No need," she said, lifting the latch to the gate. "Mateo's got it."

Mateo's fingers relaxed at her back as he followed behind her. His palm pressed against her spine as he turned to latch the gate behind them, shutting Owen out on the other side. It was all done without the two men so much as addressing each other with words.

Kailyn was sure if it had been Aldo, there would have been a scuffle on the street. Just the thought of any kind of violence made her shiver. Mateo brought his arm from her low back to wrap around her shoulder. Kailyn stopped walking at the steps to the porch, with her back to the front door. She turned to face Mateo.

"Do you want to come in?" she asked.

Mateo looked over her shoulder at the front door to her house. Then his gaze dipped as he studied her. "No."

Kailyn's stomach clenched. Her chest tightened and her limbs went heavy even as her body deflated.

"I want to ask you *out,*" he said.

"Out?"

Kailyn lifted her head. The light from the moon cast Mateo in an otherworldly glow. Stars coalesced in a pretty pattern around his dark head. Despite her whirlwind of emotions, her hands itched to reach for a set of paint and brushes.

"Out on a date," Mateo was saying. "To see if we could have a future together because…"

And here he paused and dipped his head. Mateo took both her hands in his and took a deep breath. The breath reached so far down that Kailyn thought he might have stolen some of hers away.

"Because, Kailyn, I've been in love with you for all of my past."

Yes, he had stolen some of her breath because she couldn't breathe. Kailyn's heart did that fluttery thing it only ever did for him. But it was doing that stuttery skip and not beating as it should. The effect was dizzying, and she wasn't sure she wouldn't pass out.

"What do you say?" he asked.

Kailyn said the only thing she could. She

reached up onto her tippy toes and pressed her lips to his. The kiss was brief. But only because she was seriously in danger of fainting for lack of breath.

When she broke off the kiss, they both took a heaving gasp. Kailyn still had nothing to say. Mateo didn't offer up any words of his own, just a satisfied smile. It was enough. She'd made herself clear, and he understood her perfectly.

CHAPTER TWELVE

Mateo couldn't stop touching his lower lip. It still blazed from the soft, cool touch of Kailyn's mouth. Her kiss had been fleeting, but it had left an impact.

As a soldier, Mateo had been on a plane during a storm. He'd been on a battlefield with gunfire. He'd faced hand-to-hand combat where he was outnumbered.

None of those harrowing ordeals had rocked him the way that Kailyn's kiss had.

He felt dizzy for the rest of the night. When he got up the next morning, he had to look down repeatedly to ensure his feet were touching the ground. All through the afternoon, he had to concentrate on taking deep breaths, but still the air didn't completely fill his lungs.

It hadn't bothered him this morning that the bathroom hadn't been free until well after breakfast. Mateo had debated for hours whether or not to brush his teeth last night and decided not to. He wasn't so sure he'd change his mind this morning. He was seriously contemplating never washing his face again. Or at least not until kissing Kailyn Jade became a part of his everyday routine.

He could see that future with the two of them together. It was so clear as he stood looking out at the sprawling pastures of the Flying Cross Ranch. Mateo knew this land like he knew the back of his hand.

He'd spend days when he got here as an adolescent roaming free. He knew the bend of every tree branch. He could judge the distance h"d gone by the color of the wildflowers growing beneath his feet. He could tell the time of day by which animal sounds were the loudest in his surroundings.

As he'd come to know the ranch as a kid, he'd always imagined having one person by his side on his explorations. Very soon, he'd bring Kailyn to the two trees that had grown so close together it looked as though they were hugging. He'd pick a bouquet of white, blue and yellow wildflowers for her and sit by and watch her bring the flowers to life on one of her canvases. He'd tune out the world when he cupped his hand to her cheek and brought their mouths together in a kiss that would last the entire day and into the night.

The idea of a bright and colorful and kiss-filled future thrilled Mateo so much he heard a ringing in his head. Then he realized it was his phone. The thought of Kailyn calling him had him diving to accept the call.

He put the device to his ear with a breathy, "Hello."

"Hey, bro."

Mateo realized he was still pressing his fingers to his Kailyn-kissed lips. He dropped his hand from his mouth at the sound of Aldo's voice.

"Were you eating or drinking something sweet right now? I swear I just got a sugar rush"

Mateo balled his hands into fists. This was another of those times where Aldo took their twin sense too far. If Mateo truly thought his twin could feel what it was like to kiss Kailyn, then Mateo would have to punch his brother in the mouth.

"Oh wait, it was Miguel's party last night. He made cake?"

"Yeah," Mateo confirmed. "Yeah, we all had cake." Mateo was still loathed to be singled out by his brother and their twin-sense. Sharing basic necessities with Aldo had never bothered him. It was his own experiences that Mateo wanted to keep to himself.

"You better have saved me some. From our bond, I can taste it was really sweet. Mmmm."

Mateo pursed his lips, trying to rein in his temper. He felt cold all over and wanted his brother to feel that through their twin-sense bond. Anything but the idea, the thought, even the inkling of his time with Kailyn.

"These meetings are going great. I think you'd be interested in a couple of these contracts."

"Aldo, I've already told you. I'm out. I'm staying here in Honor Valley. I'm doing the JROTC. I'm putting down roots."

Mateo didn't mention that those roots would be securely dug in around Kailyn Jade. He knew he'd have to tell his brother eventually. But not while things were new and fresh and so sweet with Kailyn. He knew Aldo would ruin it if Mateo didn't figure out how to deliver the news in a way that didn't make Aldo feel he was being cut out.

Even though Aldo was definitely being cut out of this aspect of Mateo's life.

But maybe the distance would be the best thing for announcing Mateo's new trajectory. Aldo was gone for another two days. If Mateo told him now, it would give him time to stew out of sight, and maybe he'd be calm—or at least be calmer—when he got back.

"Listen, Aldo, you should know I'm dating—"

"Andy."

Andy? Mateo didn't remember any friends they shared named Andy. Maybe Aldo had made a new friend there at the event. But Aldo wasn't the best at making new friends, especially when Mateo wasn't around.

A cloud moved overhead, and realization dawned. Aldo had used that name a lot. He'd used it as an ugly reference when they were kids. He'd pinned it on one of the two redheaded twins in their town.

"Elayne? What are you doing with Elayne Jade?"

"She's here. She's at the conference hall."

Mateo's hackles went up. The last thing he needed was for Aldo and Elayne to go nuclear when neither he nor Kailyn were around.

"Just stay away from her," Mateo said, his fingers curling around the phone.

"How can I stay away from her when she's coming right at me?"

"Look, Aldo, just—"

"Gotta go, bro. Save me some cake."

And with that, his twin cut their connection.

CHAPTER THIRTEEN

Kailyn wasn't sure how she made it through the school day. In third period, Al Morris spilled a tub of red paint on one of the worktables. The paint narrowly missed Becca Green's white jeans. Her patent leather shoes weren't so lucky, and World War III broke out. In the fifth period special needs art class, Erik Spader got hold of the glitter and... well, Kailyn made a note to give the school custodians a healthy Christmas bonus.

By some miracle of all the angels smiling down upon her, the final bell rang. Kailyn made her way around the red ravages of war on the floor on her left, hopped across a sparkling bit of linoleum on her right, and was out the door of the classroom.

The trying events of the day brushed off her shoulders and her body tensed for what was to come next. That tension was a welcome weight as she thought about what she would wear on her date with Mateo Matthews.

Unfortunately, before she got to the main doors to exit the high school, she was stopped by a low voice with high self-importance.

"I take it you won't be using school grounds as your private parking lot tonight, Ms. Jade?"

She wouldn't have turned around, except her parents had impressed upon her the need to always be kind and courteous when someone in the community spoke. Even though her parents were gone, she still wanted to curry their good will and be the best representative of the couple that had taken her and her sister in.

Kailyn put her shoulders back, plastered on a fake smile, and turned to face Owen. Before she could spew any niceties, he spoke over her. Which was typical of their time together on their two ill-fated dates.

"I don't know what's gotten into you going out in the dead of night with strange men."

Of course, this is what this would be about.

Owen didn't like competition. There should be two assistant principals in the high school. The last one had barely lasted two years, and rumors were that was because of Owen. Principal Barrow didn't complain too much, as Owen did the work of two people. But it was only because he didn't share well.

"I wasn't with a strange man. I was with Mateo Matthews. We all went to school together, remember."

"Those Matthews boys are no good. None of them know who their parents are."

Kailyn's back muscles tensed. She rolled her right shoulder as a bead of sweat trickled down her spine. Her chin lifted and her nostrils flared as she took one step toward Owen. "Is that a crack about him being a foster kid?"

For the first time since their acquaintance, Owen got a clue. His teeth pressed together as his lips twisted. He swallowed, but that didn't help whatever he'd tried to suppress from coming out of his mouth. "I'm just saying you were raised by two good Christian people. And he—"

"He was raised by a preacher who is also a decorated soldier."

Owen bit his lip. His eyes darted as he searched

for another tact. "He's using you, Kailyn. Can't you see that?"

"Using me for what? The only thing he wants that I have to give is my time and attention. And I want to give both to him."

"He's been seen with the board members. Did you know that? He's playing you."

Board members? Was this about the after school funding? Kailyn knew that both she and Mateo were still in contention for the funds. Though she hadn't thought much about that particular rivalry—especially not after that kiss last night. One of them would get the funding and the other wouldn't. She had to hope that when the board saw her amazing presentation and awarded her with their decision, that Mateo would be man enough to take it gracefully.

Kailyn had the feeling that a tall drink of water like Mateo, with muscles for days, would be strong enough to handle the rejection. And she couldn't wait to kiss it better.

"You can't be that naïve, Kailyn," Owen was saying.

"I'm seen every school day with you. You said out loud to others, including Mateo, that you were siding with me and my project."

Owen opened his mouth for more protests, but nothing came out. Kailyn didn't wait for him to think of more. She was done with the conversation. She was done with him. No more trying to remain friendly with the man. He clearly didn't understand that or the true meaning of camaraderie.

Twenty minutes later, she was standing in her bedroom, looking into her closet. She wasn't sure she had anything to wear. Nothing seemed special enough for this date with Mateo. Not that he'd seen her in any of the outfits before. And she didn't have time to go shopping.

Kailyn left her room and marched into her sisters. Running her fingers through Elayne's color-coordinated offerings was as close as going to shopping for something new that she had time for. She snatched a pale cocktail dress, along with a belt to cinch her waist and a pair of strappy heels to complete the outfit.

Even though the two were twins, Elayne had a few more curves than Kailyn. She had to fluff the dress over the belt in order to accentuate what assets she had. She might not look like Marilyn Monroe in the dress, but she didn't look like a twelve-year-old flat-chested girl either. The dress made her legs look long and what curves she had stood out. It did nicely.

By the time the doorbell rang, Kailyn was putting on the final touches of makeup. She pulled a wrap out of the closet, slipped her keys in her bag, and went to the door. A cool breeze blew into the foyer, but barely touched her because in the doorway Mateo stood broad and tall, blocking the night wind.

His gaze swept over her, leaving her heated. His lips were parted, making her hungry. His nostrils flared, causing her heart to thud against her chest. There was a spark in his eyes that made her see stars.

"Hello, Kailyn."

"Hi, Mateo."

"You are...breathtaking."

She felt breathtaking. She couldn't inhale enough to fill her lungs.

Mateo reached out his arm, crooked in an old fashion way of a Victorian gentleman. Kailyn placed her fingers on his biceps. The two of them fell into step as they walked down the path to lead to his car.

She hesitated to let him go when he opened the passenger door for her. She had to remind herself that they would be together for the rest of the night. She had to tamp down on the whisper in her heart that said she never wanted the night to end.

As they walked into the restaurant, her hand was back on his biceps. He was a sight. He wore dark slacks and a crisp white shirt and a gray jacket. It all accented his strong body and handsome face.

She saw a few women she knew. Mostly parents who were a decade older and a few familiar faces of her generation. The women's eyes roamed over Mateo as he strode confidently through the tables. When he pulled out her chair, Kailyn didn't want to let his arm go. She wanted all these women to know that this man was taken.

For his part, Mateo only had eyes for her. He only looked at her. He only smiled at her. He only seemed to notice her.

"I have to tell you again how beautiful you look in that dress," Mateo said as he refilled her wine glass.

"It's Elayne's. I don't know why I just told you that. And don't tell her. She hates when I borrow things without asking first."

Kailyn smoothed her hands down the dress as she watched Mateo fill her glass. A tremor went through his steady hands. A *clink* sounded as the wine bottle tapped the edge of the wine glass. There was a *plop* as a healthy dollop of liquid splashed into the glass before Mateo righted the bottle and set it back on the table between them.

"You haven't talked to your sister?" Mateo's gaze had been on her all night. He lowered his lids now as he reached for his own wine glass.

"Not since she left, no."

Mateo nodded. He opened his mouth and then closed it.

Kailyn got the sense that something between them had shifted. It had to be the mention of their warring siblings. This wasn't a topic they could hide from. If they were going to be together— which this night was proving to her that she wanted—then all four of them would have to find some common ground.

"It's nice to talk with another twin," Kailyn said. "I'm sure that growing up with someone who looks and sounds just like you made you yearn for and seek out your own individuality."

He glanced up then, his eyes alight with the spark that had burned when he stood gazing at her on her doorstep. In that moment, Kailyn felt the connection between them restored and stronger than before.

"Aldo wanted us to dress alike all through high school." Mateo let out a gust of air through his nose. "Going into the military was partly to soothe that side of him."

Kailyn giggled. Her adoptive parents had loved dressing her and Elayne alike, but the two of them hated it. They held their tongues because they were so grateful for the loving home, but they would strip off their matching sets once they got to school. They'd long been in the habit of stashing clothes in their lockers so they could change and be their own individual selves.

Kailyn told Mateo as much. He bemoaned the loss that he'd never thought of that idea, which made Kailyn toss her head back and laugh even more.

"That's just as beautiful as I remembered it," he said, his gaze holding hers once more.

"What is?" she asked.

"The sound of your laugh. I used to hang near the art class window to hear you laugh. I would go out of my way to pass you in the halls just for a glimpse of your smile and the possibility to hear you laugh."

"Why didn't you just come and talk to me, tell me a joke?"

"You know why."

She did. They both did. But neither of them brought up their siblings in this moment that was solely theirs.

"The main reason I came back was to see you." Mateo reached for her hand, and she gave it to him. "I want to see a lot more of you, Kailyn."

"I'd like that."

Mateo's fingers curled around hers. His fingers jerked but didn't pull from hers. A shadow moved across his face as he looked passed her shoulder. Kailyn thought it must be his brother walking toward them. But when she glanced over her shoulder, she saw an older man.

"I thought that was you, Captain Matthews."

Mateo let go of her hand and stood. He came to attention in that rigid way soldiers did when they met with someone of a higher rank. "General Jensen."

"I didn't mean to interrupt your dinner." The general gave Kailyn a friendly but dismissive smile. Then he turned back to the pudgy man in a business suit at his side. "I wanted to take a moment to introduce you to one of the investors interested in your program. Matthews is starting a JRTOC program here in the valley. He has my full support, and I think you should look at his plan to consider coming on with us."

And that's when it hit her. There was a general on the board of education. Kailyn had never met him, but she supposed she just did.

General Jensen was talking about the JROTC program like it was decided. Mateo was shaking the hand of the businessman like it was a done deal. When Mateo turned to introduce her, Kailyn didn't give him a chance. She was already out of her seat, heading for the door.

CHAPTER FOURTEEN

*E*ven though Mateo had been taught manners by all of his parents, even though the military had pounded the deference of rank into him, he marched past the general and the investor, who could potentially fund his entire business endeavor, without another glance or word. Though manners did insist that Mateo throw his credit card down onto the table before he dashed off. Disrespectful he could stand to be called, but a thief or a cheat, he could never abide.

With the bill taken care of, Mateo promptly forgot about credit security or how he'd retrieve his card. He didn't give the other guests, many of them he knew and those who knew his family, even so much as an excuse me as he whizzed past them in pursuit of his sole objective. There was only one thing he needed to retrieve this night, and it was getting away from him. If he lost Kailyn, his whole world was crashing down around him, and he would not let that happen.

Mateo was thankful for his military training in that instance. Kailyn was no match when it came to physical fitness. He would have run miles over days to catch up to her. Luckily, it only took a few strides after exiting the restaurant's door to catch up to her.

Once he had her, he had to ball his hands into fists not to grab her to him. He kept in stride with her, but she wouldn't slow down. She teetered once in her heels, and he had to grit his teeth to keep from picking her up bodily and slinging her over his shoulder.

"Kailyn, wait."

She didn't, and she teetered again.

Mateo had had enough. He reached for her, but she wrenched her arm from his hold. She looked like an avenging angel under the streetlight in that yellow dress that looked golden under the moonlight. For a second, Mateo could only stop and marvel at her beauty.

The flaring nostrils. The bright eyes. But it was the hurt in those eyes that cooled his ardor.

"He was right," she said. "He was right."

"Who was right? Kailyn, stop."

"Owen was right."

Owen? The vice principal? Mateo did not like hearing that name come from Kailyn's mouth. She had told him they'd dated during their dinner conversation, but they'd been incompatible. Mateo got the sense from the two run-ins the two men had had that Owen hadn't taken the hint about incompatibility. If Kailyn thought Owen was right about something, it would appear they'd talked again since last night.

"I can't believe I fell for it. You were playing me this whole time."

"No, I—"

"I'm so stupid. I let myself trust you."

"You can trust me."

"Really?" Finally, she stopped. She whirled on him, a finger pointing at the center of his chest.

Mateo was certain Kailyn meant that finger to be an accusatory assault. Inside his chest, his heart pounded to get to that finger and wrap itself around it. He placated the organ by taking a step closer to her so that the tip of her finger rested against his pounding chest.

"How can I trust you when you never stopped your brother from hurting my sister?"

That brought Mateo up short. His heart stopped as his mind tried to work out the implications of that statement.

"That's right. You kept quiet. Just like you're doing now, because that's what you do. You stand by quietly and let others get taken advantage of."

Kailyn's index finger curled into a ball, her other fingers surrounding it until her hand became a fist. That fist lifted an inch away from him and then came to rest against his chest. The movement was soft, but inside he felt like she'd punched right through him.

Mateo knew she was speaking of both matters at hand: the explosive history between their siblings and the after school program, which she had to think he'd stolen from her. He could let her think the worst of him about the program. But he couldn't let her thoughts about their families stand a moment longer.

"I did keep quiet," he admitted as one of his hands snaked up between them to capture her fist. "Whenever my brother and your sister went off on each other, I kept my mouth shut. My only concern was to protect you."

Kailyn opened her mouth, but Mateo rushed on to fill the silence with his truth.

"As long as the two of them fought each other, they kept you out of it."

"Your brother called me Raggedy Ann."

"No, that wasn't him." Mateo crushed her hand to his heart. With his other hand, he dared to finger the red locks that had fascinated him since the first time he'd seen her walk into the foster home. "That was me."

The betrayal on her face made his knees buckle. She turned to walk away, but he wouldn't let her go. He was never letting this woman go, not now that he finally knew what her fingers felt like wrapped up in his. Not now that he knew the texture of her hair in his palm. Not now that he knew the honey-sweet taste of her mouth against his.

"My mother had that doll. It's one of the things she brought with her when she crossed the border. It's the only thing I have left of her now, and it's my most cherished possession."

Kailyn's futile tugs against him weakened, and she gazed up into his solemn face.

"That doll had a triangle nose, pert and proud. She had button eyes, with a sparkle at the center. And her hair was made of this vibrant, red yarn."

"Your mother had a Raggedy Ann doll, and I reminded you of it?"

Mateo nodded. He watched as Kailyn struggled with this new information. On the one hand, he'd told her that she reminded him of a cherished possession. On the other hand, most didn't consider the Raggedy Ann doll to be the most attractive of toys.

"Aldo thought I was making fun of you, but I wasn't. I was a kid. I hadn't seen anything more beautiful. I didn't have anything else that I cherished more."

Kailyn swallowed. Her features softened as she regarded him. Her fist unballed. Slowly, she rotated her wrist until her fingers twined with his. Before their hands were clasped together all the way down to the webbing, she pulled back.

"The after school program?"

And now they were back around to that.

Mateo nodded. Gently, he pressed their hands together until their palms touched and they were locked in. His knuckles brushed against hers, hard calluses meeting soft skin.

"They weren't talking about the after school program in there," he said. "I withdrew my application to the board. I'm investing in commercial property to build a private program for my JROTC program."

"Wait—" She closed her eyes as though it was too much information to hear all at once. When she opened them again, her green eyes were dark with incomprehension. Yet there was also the tiny spark of hope. "We're not competing against one another?"

"No." Mateo smiled, brushing his fingertips across her brow in an effort to smooth the worry there. Like butter, it melted under his touch. "As soon as I knew you wanted the after school program, I stepped back. It's yours. You just need to make the presentation."

Her body went slack in his hold. Not as though she fainted or passed out. More like she gave up control of her body and gave it to him, like a doll that was ready to be picked up and played with.

Her chest became flush with his. Her head came to rest in the palm of his hand. Her hands slid around his neck like he was her anchor.

"I'd like to be yours, too," he said. "I don't want

to fight anymore, Kailyn. I want to be at peace. With you. But I'll fight for you if you—"

The body that had gone slack against his burst with life. Kailyn snaked her hands into his hair. With a tug that didn't take much of her strength, she pulled him down until his lips were against hers.

Now it was Mateo's body that gave up control and gave everything to her. He wrapped his arms around this woman. He picked her up off her feet and held her to him as he deepened the kiss. She was as pliant as a doll in his arms, but she was warmer and filled with life. A life that Mateo planned to spend all of his playtime in.

CHAPTER FIFTEEN

ailyn tilted her face up to the sun. The warmth of the rays was nice. The full force of the daytime star was nowhere near as nice as what it felt like to be inside Mateo's embrace. Its penetrating rays had nothing on the sensation of his lips brushing hers.

She had occupied that piece of heaven for a few hours last night after the dinner disaster. The quick goodnight kiss on Kailyn's porch steps had lingered longer and longer until the Petersons next door flicked their porch lights at the amorous couple. Too happy to be embarrassed, Kailyn finally said good night and slipped inside the front door.

She'd barely slept before the sun was up. The

new day promised more embraces and sweet kisses from Mateo. The short hands of the clock moved slowly around the dial until it was time to drive over to the Flying Cross Ranch to meet him.

A family lunch was moving fast for a second date. But she'd already been introduced, and her presence had been requested for a family day of activities this Saturday. Kailyn was spared from doing any manual chores, but the Matthews did put her to work when she arrived.

Mateo was seated next to a blonde. The girl leaned into him, looking up at him with complete adoration. Kailyn felt a spike of jealousy. Not because she thought the adolescent was going to steal her man. She just wanted to switch places with the little girl, whose name she'd learned was Daria.

Mateo gave the precocious adolescent a wink, along with an affectionate smile. Then he looked up and caught Kailyn's gaze. His grin morphed into something private, something secret, something hotter than the sun's rays.

"What's next, Ms. Jade?"

It took Kailyn a moment to focus on that voice and orient herself. She was on the porch of the Flying Cross Ranch. The five foster children were seated around her with art supplies. Some of the adults had joined too at Mateo's insistence. They were helping her prepare examples of therapeutic artwork for her presentation to the board of education.

Daria had chosen the task of drawing mandalas. Sketching the repeating patterns was very useful in regulating a person's emotions and their nervous system. The child had been a wiggly little something until Kailyn had given her instruction on how to begin. Now Daria was calm and focused on the patterns she created. Except for her glances at Mateo.

LaTisha squinted at her canvas as a caricature of herself emerged. Drawing a self-portrait was meant to mirror how a person saw themselves from the inside out. It often revealed insecurities and doubts a child, or an adult, might harbor in their souls. The petite form of that particular child didn't showcase any self-esteem issues in her broad, confident strokes. The brown-skinned girl drew herself standing in front of the White House. In the portrait, everyone around her looked much smaller, and most of them were males. LaTisha knew who she was, where she was going, and she even had a small pathway in the background indicating that she knew exactly how she was going to get there.

The little girl certainly had one of the best role models around. Savy sat leaning forward as she worked on a self-portrait of her own. The drawing was full of people. Even without a headcount, it was clear she drew her increasing family with a doting Charlie at her side.

Charlie wasn't at her side in real life. The doting husband sat on the ground leaning against Savy's legs as he glued pieces onto a mask. The pieces were all heart shapes made from the left-over scraps from the others. The making of a mask was another endeavor to reveal hard-to-express feelings. Charlie's feelings were clear about himself and about his family. He was surrounded by love, both inside and out.

"What should I do now, Ms. Jade?" asked Miguel.

Kailyn had asked Miguel and Denny to draw pictures of their emotions on a blank sheet of paper. Miguel had used every color in the crayon box to draw sunshine and rainbows. Denny hadn't drawn much, but he'd chosen blacks and grays and browns to scratch across the paper. Little did he know that said a lot about him.

"Now I want you to tear it up," said Kailyn.

That lit surprise on Denny's face. It brought a frown to Miguel's.

"Go on," Kailyn encouraged.

The boys did as instructed. Miguel tore the paper once, carefully down the middle. Then he collected the two pieces together and tore again, taking care to keep the tear as straight as possible. He likely thought he could manage to glue the pieces back together again. But once torn, things never quite fit the same way. Denny ripped his sheet to shreds.

"Now you're going to take the pieces and make something new," Kailyn went on. "Something beautiful that you plan to give to the person who means the most to you."

Miguel's smile returned, and he got to work. Denny eyed her suspiciously. He glanced at his sister and reached for the glue.

"I suppose this means our ugly emotions can be made pretty?" said Denny.

"Something like that," Kailyn agreed.

The kid gave her another suspicious side-eye, but he got to work.

That gave Kailyn a moment to make her way over to Mateo. She'd given him the family portrait assignment. Glancing at his drawing, she saw that he'd drawn himself. He was hard to mistake with that dark hair and proud chin. Two sets of gray-haired adults flanked him: one couple with light brown skin and the second with a darker Crayola shade of brown. Those must be his birth parents standing next to the Matthews. More people dotted the background: his brothers, their partners, and the children. Kailyn noted that Mateo's twin was far away from him, tucked in the corner, and without color.

The meaning was clear. Mateo no longer wanted to be identified with his twin. Kailyn's hands reached for his shoulder. Before she rested a single fingertip at his back, his pencil's movement caught her eye.

Mateo wasn't done with his artwork.

Looking closer, she saw the beginnings of a female form standing next to Mateo. When he reached for the red-colored pencil, her breath caught.

"What do you think?" he asked, holding up two red pencils. "Raspberry red? Or red orange?"

Kailyn's heart was racing too fast to let her brain form words. She was part of his portrait. She was in the picture of his life. He'd said as much last night, but seeing it on parchment somehow made it real to her.

"This is exactly the kind of activity that my wife would've loved," said Father Matthews from his rocking chair. "But she would've never gotten the boys to hold still and do much crafting."

The family's patriarch had shaken his head good-naturedly when Kailyn offered him a pad and colored pencils. Instead, he sat watching everyone with unadulterated joy on his face.

"Art can be very therapeutic if given the right conditions," Kailyn said. "They say the right brain is analytical and logical, while the left brain is where art and emotion lie. When you use art, it helps to balance the two. Especially if you're someone who tries to suppress your emotions, like a lot of kids with trauma tend to do."

Father Matthews nodded. "Seems that's something that adults could use, too. Especially soldiers back from deployment."

This wasn't the first time Kailyn had heard the idea. But she wasn't sold on it. "I'm not sure hardened soldiers and veterans would take what I do seriously."

"This one does," said Mateo. He pointed around the porch to his brothers. "So do those ones."

Charlie flashed a smile. Joe, who worked on a creation with Foxy, gave her a nod. Will hadn't picked up any craft supplies. Instead, he watched Tricksy work on a mandala. His breathing was deep and easy as his gaze tracked the motions of her colored pencil on the parchment. Topher and his girlfriend Toni hung by. Neither of them had chosen to participate, but they didn't scoff or outright disagree with their brother and father.

All in all, it wasn't an entirely glowing review of Kailyn's offerings. But it wasn't a full-on rejection. The idea of working with soldiers had some merit. Maybe someday in the future. Right now, her focus was on kids.

The Matthews kids, even with the trauma of foster homes and the later trauma of being in combat as adults, were all just fine. Mostly. They had their quirks and their tempers, but even more than that, they all had love. They had a home big enough to fit all of them. And even when the home started to burst at the seams, they made more room.

They were enjoying her art projects. It was revealing parts of themselves they might not have vocalized. But deep down, this large family, by choice if not blood, knew that no matter what, they were going to be okay.

Standing amongst them, Kailyn let the feeling wash over her. She'd had love in her life. The love of her sister was ever present, if sometimes annoying. The love of her adoptive parents was still a warm shawl over her shoulders. But this big love… well, this was something that a girl could get used to.

A big arm came around her waist. That arm said she was included. That arm said she was wanted. Just as Kailyn made up her mind to burrow into that embrace and take the owner of the arm up on his offer, Mateo stiffened and let her go.

When she looked up into his face, gone was the welcoming light in his eyes. Gone was the open gaze that offered her a future. Following the line of Mateo's gaze, Kailyn saw a car ambling down the drive. When it came to a stop, an identical replica of Mateo climbed out.

Except this Mateo was frowning. Because that wasn't her Mateo. Aldo had come home early.

"What's Raggedy Ann doing here?"

CHAPTER SIXTEEN

Mateo's hand on Kailyn's back felt like the start of something. No, not the start. He had always had a foot over the starting line where it came to this particular girl. He had just been waiting for his chance to take off at a sprinting pace. The moment she smiled at him a couple of days ago, Mateo had heard the resounding blast from a starting pistol—and he was off.

He felt like he was running the ace of his life, and it was all moving too slowly for him. His heart had been pounding out a fast-paced rhythm the last few days, but Mateo barely felt the impact of his feet on the ground. Now Kailyn was finally catching up with him. His head was so far in the clouds with the plans he was making for a future with this woman that he could see clear into the next year, the next decade, and beyond. With his hand at Kailyn's back, Mateo planned to run with her for the rest of his life.

For now, he held still as his family took in the two of them. His father's looks were approving. His sisters-in-law wore those calculating expressions as though they were sizing Kailyn up for a bridal gown. His brothers, on the other hand, had taken one look at the two of them together, then commenced with giving each other those speaking glances that annoyed Mateo so much.

Once upon a time, Mateo had been on the other end of those glances. He would look over at his twin and roll his eyes when Charlie and Savy snuck off together. Both he and Aldo would lift a brow whenever Joe snuck a glance at Foxy. The twins would frown in tandem whenever Will took a step back from Tricksy in order to let Topher step forward. Now those lovestruck men all traded smirks as they watched Mateo stake his claim on Kailyn.

This time, when Mateo caught his brother's eye after Aldo hopped out of his car, they frowned at each other. But it was Aldo who rolled his eyes while frowning and then completed his repertoire of facial expressions with a raised eyebrow.

"What's Raggedy Ann doing here?"

Mateo had been so focused on Kailyn that he hadn't heard the sound of tires kicking up dirt coming toward them. He'd been too fixated on the strands of gold nestled in her red locks to hear the tires screech when Aldo put the car in park. Not even the slam of the car door called to him. Not even the call of his twin's name by the young kids getting up off the porch to launch themselves at the newcomer.

But those five words did.

Not for the first time, Mateo realized how much Kailyn Jade reminded him of his mother's prized possession. Kailyn's hair was that same bright, vibrant red as the doll's. Her nose was lifted into the air with the same perky tilt. The round buttons of her eyes had the same sparkle.

Except the spark was slowing going out of Kailyn's eyes. His red-haired beauty's cheeks were flaming with a blush. Her lips were pinched. Her body was tense.

Mateo looked again at his reflection. Aldo was glaring at him. In his brother's eyes, Mateo saw that there was no fascination with the antique doll.

Aldo didn't see the beauty of his mother's treasure, nor the woman that Mateo treasured. When Aldo said the name, it was an insult, not an endearment.

"You don't get to call her that," said Mateo.

Aldo's gaze narrowed on his brother. Just as there had been wordless communication between the other Matthews boys moments ago, the twins engaged in a silent conversation. The corner of Aldo's eye twitched in a belligerent question. Mateo's answer was broadcast loudly in the compression of his lips into a thin, implacable line.

Mateo knew the silence would be short-lived. Aldo, who could rarely keep his mouth shut during a confrontation, would retaliate with words that would likely hurt Kailyn. And then Mateo would have to knock his brother's teeth loose.

True to form, Aldo parted his lips.

Mateo tensed. The hand that rested at Kailyn's back opened and closed. He wanted to keep his hold on her, but he had to be prepared to launch at his brother. His knuckles cracked with indecision.

Aldo's gaze flicked to Kailyn, and then he spewed words that Mateo could never imagine hearing him say. "I'm sorry, Kailyn."

The silence on the ranch was so complete. Mateo couldn't even hear his own heartbeat because he'd gone so still. He couldn't have heard what he thought he just did.

Kailyn blinked hard. Then she blinked again. She rubbed her ear for good measure. She wasn't the only one. All around, his brothers and sisters tugged their earlobes or rubbed at their foreheads as though trying to reset a phone or computer screen.

"I've had a trying couple of days," Aldo continued. "I shouldn't have taken it out on you."

Mateo's instinct was to go to his brother and ask what was wrong, because he knew something was wrong. He didn't need his twin-sense to know. It wasn't just the unexpected apology, nor the fact that Aldo had backed down from a fight.

There were bags under his eyes. His hair was out of place, like he'd run his hands through it one too many times. His shirt was wrinkled, and there were a couple of scuffs on his shoes. Not normal behavior for a man who had just left the military and come from a military contract interview. Not normal behavior from one of Captain Haran Matthews' sons.

"You okay, Al?" Charlie spoke the words that had caught in Mateo's throat.

Aldo shrugged. His gaze didn't meet anybody's.

Instead, he leaned back and looked up at the sky.

"Things work out with any of the military contractors?"

"Yeah, but I'm no longer interested in that work," Aldo said, his gaze still unfocused and not landing on anyone in particular. "I'm gonna stay home."

"That's good news, son," said Father Matthews. "What will you do instead?"

Aldo looked to Mateo. Mateo held his breath.

This was not the plan. The plan was for Aldo to go and give Mateo a break to be his own man and not a twin. If Aldo stayed and tried to work in the JROTC program, that would interfere with his social and professional life.

"I don't know," Aldo said finally. He looked lost. "I need to figure some stuff out."

"You should get Ms. Jade's help," said Miguel. "She's really good at helping you figure out your insides and your outsides."

"I don't need Elayne Jade's help," Aldo snapped.

The absolute silence track made a repeat appearance. Only this time, Mateo heard a low hiss from the woman standing next to him.

"If you ask me, she's the one that needs therapy to deal with all that baggage she carries around."

"Hey, that's my sister you're talking about," said Kailyn, taking a step forward. "And if she has any baggage, it's because you put it there."

"Me? What have I ever done to her?" Aldo put his foot on the first step up the porch.

"Are you serious?" Kailyn took one step down the porch.

Mateo rushed down a couple of steps to stand between the two of them. It was a position he never wanted to be in—his hands outstretched between his brother and the woman he wanted to spend the rest of his life with.

"Mateo, tell your brother to back off my sister," said Kailyn. Mateo's fingertips brushed the cotton of her shirt over the spot where her heart beat out a rapid pace.

Aldo stepped right up to Mateo's other hand, his chest heaving with passion. "Mateo tell your... Wait? What is she to you?"

"She's my..." And there Mateo faltered.

He couldn't say *She's my everything*. She was more than a girlfriend. With his arms outstretched, trying to hold off World War III and his heart in his throat, that left his tongue tied. His hesitancy made both Aldo's and Kailyn's gazes narrow on him.

CHAPTER SEVENTEEN

Kailyn had never had the occasion to hate anyone or anything. Aldo Matthews had always been the closest thing to that line that she never crossed. Today, that childish man had taken enough steps for her to cross it.

She had never found a single thing to like about Aldo other than his face. His face which was so like his brother's. But now, upon closer inspection, the identical twins looked absolutely nothing alike. There were frown lines at the corners of Aldo's eyes. Mateo had the same lines at the corners of his eyes, but they were from perpetually smiling.

Aldo's nose was long and proud. But his nose looked slightly crooked. Likely because it had been punched a few times when his mouth got him into trouble.

The brothers had the same mouth. Kailyn was sure that if she took a measuring stick to their lips, she'd find the exact same proportions across both males. The difference would likely be slight, but the visual sight was clear enough for her to see the stark differences. Aldo's lips rested in a grimace where Mateo's, even when he wasn't actively smiling, curled slightly, ready to grin at any moment.

No, the Matthews twins couldn't have looked more different to her. But the biggest tell was that Aldo, for some reason, spewed hatred whenever it came to her sister. Even when she wasn't there to defend herself. Well, too bad for Aldo that Kailyn was there to defend her sister, if no one else would.

Kailyn was not a fighter. She hated fighting. But enough was enough.

She had one last card to play. She looked to Mateo. He had been her silent champion when it came to Owen. Silent and steady. Without raising a fist, he'd run Owen out of her life—her personal life, at any rate. If anyone could get his brother to ease up on her sister, then he could. He had to.

Mateo had proven himself level-headed. He would smooth this out by talking to his brother.

Every time Aldo and Elayne had clashed in the past, Mateo may have stood off to the side without a word, but if Kailyn asked him to say something, to step in, she knew that he would. She just needed to ask him.

"Mateo, tell your brother to back off my sister," said Kailyn, her voice filled with the calm she reached for. The calm that always came over her when Mateo was near.

"Mateo, tell your..." And there Aldo paused. His cruel face contorted into confusion as he looked between her and his twin. "What is she to you?"

"She's my..."

There were so many words Mateo could have used to fill the end of that sentence. He could've said *friend*. Kailyn would've been disappointed at that low-rung categorization. But in reality, the two of them had only been on two dates. Technically, only one, as she wasn't sure this counted as an actual date since his family had put her to work.

If he had said *girlfriend,* that would've made her heart skip a beat, sure. But it was only a couple of rungs higher up on the relationship ladder. For Kailyn, their relationship felt like it had reached higher ground. She knew in her heart that she wanted to go all the way to the top with Mateo.

But then he paused… and she felt herself slip on the ladder that they'd begun to climb together.

Mateo didn't know what she was to him? She knew exactly what he was to her. He was the man that stole her breath. He was the man that had her heart skip beats. He was the man she was falling in love with.

No, falling was the wrong tense. She had fallen for him a long time ago. Likely when they were kids, and he'd smiled at her that first time. She had been free falling for years now. Right now, she felt the thud of the impact. It wasn't gentle.

"I think they're going to get married."

All adults turned sharp gazes back to the porch. They all faced toward Foxy. But the self-proclaimed psychic hadn't been the one to voice that opinion. It had been Miguel.

"Isn't that right, Ms. Foxy?" said Miguel. "Can't you see it?"

Foxy cocked her head to the side and regarded Mateo and Kailyn. A slow smile broke across her face, but she neither confirmed nor denied Miguel's claim.

There was a fluttering in Kailyn's belly as she took in the exchange between Miguel, with his vociferous claim, and Foxy, with her silent acknowledgment. Her knees felt weak as she stood on the porch steps with the realization that she wasn't the only one who saw the steep climb up the relationship ladder that was laid out for her and Mateo.

The question was, would Mateo take that climb with her?

Kailyn bit at her bottom lip. When she looked up, Mateo's gaze tracked the motion. Slowly, his hands lowered until they rested at his side. He turned his back on his brother and faced her fully. He lifted one foot, placing it on the porch step just below hers. His hand reached for her, palm up this time instead of outstretched in a stop-in-the-name-of-love motion. His open palm asked her to come to him in the name of love. Kailyn lifted her hand to meet his, but that's when Aldo interrupted them again.

"That would be the biggest mistake of your life," said Aldo.

Mateo dropped his hand as though it had been scalded by fire. His face morphed until it looked like his brother's. Gone were the soft lines at the corners of his eyes. Gone were the groves at the corner of his mouth that always formed his smile.

Anger lit Mateo's face. His hand balled into a

fist. Kailyn reached for him, but it was too late. He swung, adding another dent to that crooked nose and making him and his twin brother look even more different.

The sound of bone meeting bone turned Kailyn's stomach. The sight of blood when Aldo's head snapped back made her recoil. The two men were a blur as they continued to trade blows. Kailyn could no longer tell Mateo from Aldo as they went down to the ground in grunts and groans.

The sight of the violence was more than she could handle. She took a step back as the brothers tussled in front of her. When the other Matthewses dove into the fray, she stepped to the side. Kailyn kept walking until she was on the other side of the fight. She kept going until she'd reached her car in the drive. She placed her keys in the ignition and then she was driving away until the sound of angry shouts and the sight of brutality was no longer in her rearview mirror.

CHAPTER EIGHTEEN

Mateo let his arm swing. The defensive move was wide—wide enough that an opponent a mile away would see it coming. Aldo could've blocked it. He had plenty of time to step out of Mateo's path. Instead of moving or deflecting the punch, Aldo closed his eyes and tilted up his chin.

That action sent a shockwave through Mateo. It shook him as fiercely as an uppercut would have. Why wasn't Aldo fighting back? The man never backed down from a fight. Especially when it involved Elayne Jade.

But this fight wasn't about Elayne. It was about Kailyn.

No, scratch that. This fight was about Aldo and

how he would need to mind his tongue and respect boundaries if he was going to have any hope of maintaining a place in Mateo's life. Because Kailyn was his number one priority right now.

In the space of Mateo coming to that realization, his other brothers had the time to catch his wayward punch before it could connect. Joe and Charlie each grabbed one of Mateo's arms, while Will and Topher did the same to an eerily compliant Aldo.

It took Aldo another second and a long sigh before he opened his eyes. Mateo wasn't sure what to do with the turmoil of emotion he saw reflected back at him in eyes that were a mirror image of his. He didn't have time to unravel what was going on with his brother. He had to clean up the mess Aldo had made in front of Kailyn.

Mateo tried to turn around, but Charlie and Joe had him on lockdown. Glancing over his shoulder, he didn't see Kailyn where he'd left her. He jerked his head to the right, expecting to see her huddled with Savy and her sisters. But Kailyn wasn't there either.

The children were all huddled together at the end of the porch. Denny stood protectively in front of the wide-eyed bunch. The protective stance of the teenager, along with the look of betrayal in his gaze, colored Mateo's cheeks with shame. He'd have to fix that, but first he had to fix things with Kailyn.

Mateo turned back to face the front... and that's when he saw her.

Dirt kicked up from her tires as she drove out of the gates to the Flying Cross Ranch. Mateo lifted his foot to catch up the distance between them. His legs assured him he could keep pace with her car as it pulled out onto the two-lane street. The steel traps around his arms and shoulders and biceps begged to differ.

"Not until you calm down, bro."

Charlie's voice and his hold could only deter Mateo so much. With Joe's added strength, Mateo knew he was grounded. He could only watch as Kailyn and her car faded from his view. When next he looked over his shoulder, he found his father's gaze.

Father Matthews didn't look angry. He didn't even look at Mateo. His gaze was on the cloud of dust left by the car retreating from his home.

Haran Matthews did not condone fighting. He preferred his sons to talk matters out. But he also knew that boys would be boys, and if they hurt each other, he expected them to patch each other up.

His father reached into his pocket and pulled out a pristine white handkerchief. He handed the cloth to Mateo. "Clean your brother up."

The white cloth acted like a flag of surrender. Joe and Charlie let go of Mateo's arms. Topher and Will did the same to Aldo. Aldo still didn't raise his head to look at his twin. He didn't need to for Mateo to see the trickle of blood from where his fist had connected.

"With all due respect, Father, I think I should go after Kailyn. She's the one that was hurt the worst."

"You shouldn't go after her in this state," said his father, waving his hand at Mateo's chest.

Looking down, Mateo saw that there were a few spots of blood on his shirt. Not only that, but his pants had collected dirt. He looked like he'd rolled in mud with a pig. In reality, he just had.

"Uncle Mateo," said Miguel, "Ms. Jade doesn't like fist fighting. You should've used your words."

Here he was being chastised like a child, by a child, when it was Aldo who started it. It was always Aldo who started things. And always

Mateo, who had to pay the price. Well, he was done.

Aldo sat on the bottom of the porch stairs. Savy snatched the cloth from Mateo and knelt beside him to fuss over his bloody lip. He didn't wince when Savy put the cloth to his mouth. Aldo didn't budge when Mateo stepped in front of him. Aldo hadn't even thrown a punch back at Mateo in that fight. He hadn't even defended himself. It was very unlike him.

"I'm fine," Mateo said, shrugging off Charlie's hand when he went to hold him back. "I just want to talk to him."

His brothers gave him a doubtful look as they crowded around the twins. For his part, Aldo ignored his brothers and reached for a piece of paper that had fallen down the steps of the porch. It was Mateo's drawing. A drop of blood splattered on the edge. Mateo yanked the artwork from his brother's hands. His thumb smudged the blood, pressing the unwanted coloration into the corner of his handiwork. He blotted at the blood, but he doubted it would come out.

Aldo kept his gaze forward. There definitely was something off with his brother. But Mateo's first concern had to be Kailyn.

"You owe her an apology," said Mateo.

Aldo blew through his nose. His lip curled into something that looked like a smile, but it had no joy in it.

"She's in my life now."

"I can see that." Aldo motioned to the painting. "Meanwhile, I've been put in the shadows."

Red was the most vibrant color in the painting. It was vivid in the loops and curls that were Kailyn's hair. It was true that Aldo was placed in the back. But he was just as colorless as the other people in Mateo's life. Because for Mateo, it was Kailyn that shone brightest.

"We were born together," Mateo began. "You're close to me. But it's time to let others get closer to us. It's time for us to be individuals."

Aldo lifted his head. Mateo saw dark circles under his eyes. It not only looked like his brother hadn't rested in a while; it looked like a light inside of him had gone out.

"You think I can't be by myself?" said Aldo. "You think I can't make my own decisions?"

"I think you like having me there. But I want to be with her."

"Well"—Aldo stood and brushed his hands down his pants—"you can't be with her."

Aldo turned to head up the steps, but Mateo grabbed his shoulder. From the corner of his eye, he saw his brothers move in. Mateo let his twin go and held up his hands.

"I'm still using my words," said Mateo. "But he needs to shake out of this—whatever this is."

"You're the one that needs to shake it off, bro." Aldo jabbed his finger at Mateo's chest. "You can't be with Kailyn because she's your sister."

For the third time that afternoon, a total silence descended upon the Flying Cross Ranch. There definitely was something very wrong here. Mateo and Aldo didn't have any other biological siblings. Their parents had wanted more, but they hadn't been blessed before they had graduated to glory.

Aldo scrubbed his hands through his hair and down his face. When he got to his mouth, he winced as his callused fingers brushed against his busted lip. "Yesterday, I... I kinda got married."

Mateo took a step back. He bumped into the broad chest of Charlie as his brothers all moved in closer.

"Married?" asked Joe.

"To who?" asked Charlie.

Mateo felt like he knew the answer to this question, but it seemed impossible. It was unimaginable. By the looks on all the adult faces surrounding them, it was clear they'd all come to the same conclusion. So no one was surprised when Aldo said the name.

"To Elayne Jade."

In this fourth silence, even the insects hushed. Not a cricket chirped. Not a bird tweeted.

"We got drunk and… and it just happen"d."

As the silence continued, the ants halted their march beneath the porch steps at the shocking news. The squirrels stood at attention, clutching their acorns and nuts against their chests as though they were clutching their pearl".

"That doesn't make me and Kailyn blood relations."

It was the only thing Mateo could think to say. It was the only piece of logic that he could grasp on to. Except… there was one other undeniable, irrefutable truth in this situation.

"Aldo, you don't drink."

CHAPTER NINETEEN

"Oh, I can totally believe every word you just said. Aldo Matthews is a conniving, lying, trickster and I can't wait for him to leave this town and leave us in peace."

Kailyn hadn't said any of those things to her sister. In fact, she had been very judicious in her description of the events of earlier that afternoon once she'd arrived home and found her sister pacing the living room. Elayne was still pacing the length of the living room floor now as she got herself worked up.

Elayne was barefoot, but the impact of her heels striking the floor brought to mind a booted army storming the capitol. Her rigid shoulders brought to mind a general preparing to give the final order to decimate the opposition. Her curled lip looked like a devil who would enjoy glaring down at all the carnage he'd been a party in creating.

Elayne did not look like herself.

"That family is nothing but a bunch of brutes," Elayne went on. She punched her fist in the air and pointed her finger to punctuate her statements. It was a pretty brief statement, but her hand gestures continued long after she'd stopped talking. She did not stop pacing.

"I don't think you're being fair," said Kailyn. "The Matthews are decent people as a whole. There's only really one bad apple in that bunch."

Elayne came to an abrupt halt in her pacing and rounded on Kailyn. "I thought you said Mateo threw the first punch."

Kailyn recoiled at the accusation hurled at her. "Only because Aldo insulted me."

One by one, Elayne curled her fingers into her palm until they were a tight fist. "I just wish I could have been there to see him go down. No—no, I wish I could've been the one to punch him in that proud nose of his. He thinks he's so handsome."

Elayne had stopped her forward march. Now she stood with her legs braced. The pounding continued as she punched her closed fist into her open palm. Her gaze went wistful, as though she was picturing that proud nose on that handsome face as she continued to punch into the center of her hand.

"Wait a minute." Elayne's attention came back to Kailyn. "What were you doing behind enemy lines in the first place?"

"They're not our enemy."

"Oh, you naïve girl. He's finally gotten to you, hasn't he?"

"What? Who?"

"Don't play dumb, Kailyn. I've seen the way Mateo Matthews used to look at you when we were kids. He was all puppy dog eyes while his brother was a pit bull."

Kailyn pressed her lips together because that was the truth of it. Mateo had gotten to her. He'd gotten inside her head. He'd gotten inside her heart.

She did not condone violence. It made her beyond uncomfortable. But maybe she should have stayed and talked it out with Mateo instead of coming home to Elayne.

"They're playing some kind of game with us," said Elayne.

"Who?"

Elayne threw back her head and let out an annoyed huff. "The Matthews twins."

"Mateo isn't playing with me. He has feelings for me. He said he has for a long time."

For a moment, Elayne simply stared at her sister. Even though they had the same eyes, Kailyn couldn't decipher exactly what was in her sister's green gaze. When Elayne finally spoke, her voice was a snarl.

"Aldo said the same thing to me."

"Aldo? You had a conversation with Aldo?"

Elayne's face softened for one whole second. And then it iced over. She turned away from Kailyn and began to pace again.

"Elayne?"

"I hate him." She flounced down into a chair and turned away, but not before she dabbed at her eyes. "I just hate him so much. I wish the earth would just open up and swallow him whole. But then it probably would spit him back out because the man is so distasteful."

Elayne's last words were barely intelligible because they were said on the tail end of a sob. That sob became a hiccup. Once the hiccup cleared, Elayne began to cry in earnest.

Kailyn felt the sharp pain in her chest before her sister began to rub there. She felt a tightness in her throat as Elayne sobbed uncontrollably. Even as she rushed over to her twin to wrap her arms around the shaking form, Kailyn felt the weight of the world descend on her shoulders.

She tried to squeeze her sister tight and take on some of the burden. Kailyn just wasn't sure what she was lifting from her sister's heart.

"He tricked me, Kailyn."

"Who tricked you? Aldo?"

Elayne sniffled as she nodded her head. "And I fell for it."

"What did you fall for? What did he do?"

"Aldo Matthews tricked me into marrying him."

The weight Kailyn had been trying to take from Elayne forced Kailyn back on her haunches. Her world spun around. Up was down. Right was left. In was out.

Elayne had married Aldo Matthews?

"I told him I wanted to annul it immediately." Elayne shrugged off Kailyn's touch and straightened her shoulders. "He said no."

Kailyn wanted to speak. To ask questions. To get answers. To make her world stop spinning. But she was having difficulty swallowing due to the lump in her throat.

"He thinks he's got me cornered for..." Elayne swiped angrily at the tears falling down her cheeks. "For whatever game he's trying to play. But I'm going to make his life miserable until he does give me that annulment and end this sham of a marriage."

CHAPTER TWENTY

Mateo's wrist worked as he polished his shoes. It didn't take a healthy amount of elbow grease before he could see himself in the shine. From the gleam of his shoe, a stranger looked back at him dressed in uniform.

All his life he'd done nothing but love this country. From his birth parents' reverence of it, to his adoptive parents' devotion to it. He had been proud to enlist to serve this union, which had given him so much. Though he had retired from service, he intended to continue to serve.

Straightening to his full height, Mateo saw his mirror image, though there was no reflective glass in the family room. Aldo wore the same uniform, the same medals, but he and his twin did not look the same this morning.

Aldo looked old and tired. He also looked determined. That determination was the only other thing besides their uniform that the brothers had in common today. Unfortunately for Aldo, this was one battle he was going to lose.

"You're not coming," said Mateo as he bent down to put on his shoes.

"Yes, I am."

Mateo gave a decisive shake of his head. Aldo said nothing. Nor did Mateo see his brother walk away in his polished shoes. When he straightened, Aldo put up his hands.

"I owe her an apology," said Aldo. "Kailyn, I mean. She's important to you."

Mateo opened his mouth to deny his brother, but as he took in the sight of his twin, he paused. Aldo's shoulders should have been straight. Instead, they drooped. His gaze should have been direct and his chin high at attention. Yet his jaw was visibly clenched, and bags weighed his eyes.

"What if Elayne's there?" asked Mateo.

Aldo turned away until his face was in profile. But he couldn't hide the turmoil that pinched the corner of his mouth and lowered his eyelids to half mast. He opened his mouth, but nothing came out except a weary sigh.

Mateo knew that sigh. It had come from his chest all night long as he waited for the sun to rise on this day—this day where he could finally do what he did best and take action. Aldo had been tightlipped about what happened between him and Elayne and their impromptu marriage. But his brother had sighed a great deal since returning home from his adventure.

"Just promise not to cause a scene," said Mateo.

"When do I ever cause a scene?"

Instead of answering that rhetorical question, Mateo marched past his brother. He was certain there would be a scene. There always was whenever Aldo and Elayne were in the same room together. But no one could have ever written the drama that had unfolded when none of them were looking at those two. Mateo had a strong notion that Aldo didn't want the curtain to fall on whatever they were playing at.

"I'm glad the two of you made up," said Father Matthews. Their father looked up at his two sons with pride in his eyes as they stepped out onto the porch.

It was a warm day on the ranch. A slight breeze

blew through the trees. The children milled about doing their chores as it was a teacher workday and they were out of school. Being out of school did not mean a day off for the Matthews brood.

Denny and LaTisha lugged a bale of hay into the horse stalls. The two chatted amiably as they got to work. Miguel and Daria laughed as Ashton wiggled his thin body in a dance move over in the garden.

"You thought that was a fight?" Aldo was saying. "We caused more damage to each other on the playground as kids."

Father Matthews sighed, but there was a grin touching his lips as he did so.

"We're good, Dad," said Mateo. "This knuckle-head is just coming along to give moral support."

"And to class up the place," said Aldo. "Everyone knows I look good in my uniform."

"We have the same face, you know," said Mateo.

"I've been thinking about wearing another uniform," Aldo said. "I know the town police force is hiring."

That statement lifted the weight off of Mateo's heart. It looked like Aldo was feeling the need for some space of his own. His twin was finally coming to terms with his need to be an individual.

Perhaps that was due to whatever was going on between him and Elayne. Mateo knew he wanted his own space to make room for Kailyn. Because he was determined that she would be in his life. And he had just the plan to make that happen.

With all of his investors lined up in under a week, Mateo had already secured the space for the new JROTC program. They were set to move into the place in just a matter of weeks. Mateo tucked the plans in his bag and climbed into the car to head to the Board of Education meeting.

He'd given Kailyn time to cool off. Today was the day of her presentation. He wasn't entirely sure if she wanted him there, but he wouldn't miss it for the world. Besides, he had a very important question he needed to ask her. One that would change both of their lives if she said yes.

When he walked into the small conference room appointed for school board meetings, she was the first thing he saw. She had always been a beacon for him, from her brief time at the foster care home to their years in school together. Even when he had enlisted and she'd stayed local, he'd kept tabs on her. Now he wanted to get and keep his arms around this woman.

He especially wanted to hold her now as she

wrung her hands. Was she nervous? He couldn't imagine why. She had this in the bag. He'd eliminated all competition so that she could have exactly what she wanted. Mateo planned to pull that particular move for the rest of their lives, which he hoped they would spend together.

Kailyn gave her fingers a shake. She rolled her shoulders back, taking in a deep breath. When her gaze lifted, it fixed on him.

Mateo's heart stopped. His whole body held still as she regarded him. She wasn't frowning. She looked bewildered, as if his presence was unexpected.

His heartbeat picked up again when her gaze softened and she breathed a visible sigh of relief. She didn't take a step toward him. She couldn't as she was standing at the presentation podium. But she did hold his gaze for a few seconds.

Mateo smiled brightly at her. In that smile, he tried to communicate encouragement. He wanted to remind her of how strong she was. How deserving she was for this program of hers to get funded. He wanted to mouth the words *I love you*. But he didn't dare go that far. At best, it would throw her off her game.

The meeting was called to order. Kailyn turned

to face the board, who were all gathered in a semi-circle at the front of the room. General Jensen sat just off to the right. He gave Mateo a nod before turning his attention to the presentation screen.

There were a few stammers as Kailyn began. But each time she looked up and caught his gaze, she found her way again. The presentation ended with polite applause. The vote was taken immediately. The ayes were unanimous. The funding was hers.

Kailyn stood at the podium, stunned. In front of her, the board members rose from their seats to come down and congratulate her. Around the room in the audience, town members and concerned parents lined up behind the podium, prepared to discuss the issues they felt with the school curriculum, testing procedures, and accommodations for their children.

Before long, Kailyn stood by herself. Her lips were still parted in that O of surprise that things had gone her way. Had she truly expected that she would have to fight for anything she wanted? Not while he was around. He would fight this woman's every battle so that she could spend all her time spreading her peaceful art over the ugliness of the world.

"Hi," Mateo said after she stepped out of the door to the conference room.

"Hello," she said as she let the door close behind her.

"I'm sorry about the other day. I should've handled that better."

"I should have stayed and discussed my feelings with you."

Mateo half smiled, half grimaced. If any other woman, or any other person, had mentioned the need to discuss feelings with him, he would have run for the hills. For this woman, he wanted to know her every thought and emotion.

"Congratulations," he said, motioning to the now blank presentation board.

"I feel like I just added a lot more work to my plate without much compensation. But I know it'll be worth it."

"About that—I have a proposal I want to run by you."

"A… a proposal." Her lower lip trembled as she sounded out the second word.

"It's one that would have us spending a lot of time together for the near future."

"It would?" Kailyn pressed her right hand to her heart.

Mateo took a step closer to her. He reached up with trembling fingers of his own and placed them over hers. "But I think it's the right decision, and there's no one else I would dream of asking."

"Ask me."

For a moment, Mateo forgot the question he had planned to ask her. His heart was demanding he ask her a very different question. Mateo pulled the paperwork from his bag. He didn't present it to her just yet. Instead, he held it between them.

"Kailyn Jade""

"Yes, Mateo?"

"Would you be my…"

"Would I be your…? What?"

"Would you come work at my program and be my art therapist?"

CHAPTER TWENTY-ONE

Kailyn had lost her breath. Her heart was racing so fast as Mateo posed his question to her. He was going to ask her The Question.

Could this day get any better? No, she didn't think it was possible.

Her presentation had gone off without a hitch. Well, no, that wasn't entirely true either. Her voice had hitched more times than she cared to admit. Each time she got nervous and lost her way in her prepared remarks, she'd only needed to glance over at Mateo, and she'd felt a surge of confidence. A surge of certainty. It was what she was feeling now as he prepared to pose his question to her.

She knew it was too soon for that particular

question. Her life was about to change with added work. She was taking on more responsibility now that her after school program was being fully funded by the school board. There would be supplies to buy and lessons to plan and advertising to get kids interested in what art therapy could offer them.

It would be an uphill battle. But she wanted to take the trek. And taking a trek with a ring on her finger and this man at her back sounded like the smartest thing she could do.

They'd barely gotten past their first fight. But the mere fact that they were standing face to face after he'd gotten physical and she'd run away had to mean that they could work out anything that came their way.

He'd come for her today. He'd come and stood by her, lending his silent strength even after she'd run away from the problem.

Kailyn realized that Mateo's silence all the years that they were children hadn't been complacence. He'd been protecting her even then. So long as their siblings were focused on battling one another, none of their ire could reach the two of them. The only time Mateo had ever spoken up was when the verbal battle had come too close to her. Like the other day.

This man would fight for her if she needed him to. He would do it with silence, with words, or with his fists. Kailyn didn't want Mateo to fight. Not for her. Not with her.

Kailyn loved Mateo. She loved him deeply. Likely had since the first time she'd laid eyes on him. That feeling, that knowledge, brought her peace. Peace was the only thing she wanted from him. So when he asked his question, she knew she was going to say yes. Almost before he got the words out of his mouth, she was saying it.

"Yes. Yes! Wait. What?"

Mateo hadn't said the word *wife*. He'd asked her to be his *art therapist*. To come and work for him? To be his employee?

"You made me see the value of what you do," said Mateo. "Savy usually has to threaten the kids to get them to sit still or get up and do something. You had them all in line with the art. You made it okay for them to uncover and focus on their emotions. I think this could be really valuable to those about to go into the military, as well as those currently in the armed forces, or those who have finished their service. I think you could make a real difference with them, like you have with me."

It wasn't what Kailyn was expecting to hear from him. But it was exactly what she needed to hear. It was exactly what she wanted to do. She did want to help those warriors who were prepared to fight or who came home battered and bruise on the inside or out to find the peace that she found in Mateo's silent embrace.

"Yes," she said again, a bit more sedately this time.

"Also—" Mateo stepped forward, his voice going quiet so that only she could hear. "I'd like to take you out again on another date."

"Yes," she said.

"Not just one date. I'd like to monopolize as much of your time as I can manage."

"Yes."

"And then, sometime in the near future, at a more appropriate time, I'd like to ask you another big question."

"Yes."

Kailyn took a deep breath in. As she breathed out, Mateo inhaled. He inhaled her relief. He inhaled her joy. He inhaled the beginnings of their future together.

With his hand still over hers and her hand on her heart, Mateo leaned in. Kailyn tilted her head back to receive his kiss. Before his lips could connect with hers, yelling interrupted them. Those raised voices were all too familiar.

"I don't know what game you're playing at, Aldo Matthews, but I'm going to make you regret it."

"You think I could regret anything more than finding myself hitched to you?"

"Well, there's an easy fix to that." Elayne shoved a paper clipped stack of documents against Aldo's chest. "Just sign the annulment papers."

Aldo stepped back from the papers as though they'd burned his chest. His nose scrunched as though he smelled something foul.

"Well? What are you waiting for?" Elayne demanded. "You want to be rid of me, don't you? Sign the papers."

Elayne let go of the pages. Aldo reached for them too late. A number of pagers slipped free of the paperclip and wafted to the floor. Somehow the paperclip had gotten wrapped around Elayne's red hair, which had come loose from her bun.

Aldo reached up to snag the metallic clip. When he did so, his fingertips brushed against Elayne's check. Her inhale of breath was audible from across the hall.

Elayne's lips parted. Aldo's did the same. He gave a tug, and the paperclip came loose. He held it between them as they stood in a puddle of divorce papers.

The sound of arguing wafted from the closed door of the conference room, likely some parent unhappy with the board's decision and how it was affecting their child. The raised voice snapped Elayne from her stupor. Without another word, she stepped away from Aldo and stormed past him to the exterior doors.

Aldo stood watching her go, paperclip still in hand and annulment pages in disarray at his feet.

"Those two need to get that annulment," said Mateo. "And fast."

"They're not going to get an annulment," Kailyn said.

"They can't stand each other."

"I don't know." There was certainty in her voice. But her tone was still tinged with worry. "Your brother seems to like tugging my sister's hair."

"Isn't that a bad thing?"

Aldo and Elayne clearly had a whirlwind around them. It was a weather system Kailyn wasn't interested in. She much preferred the warm sunshine of Mateo's embrace. Though they had already proven that a little stormy weather wasn't enough to tear them apart.

"I don't know," she said, twining her arms around his neck. "Try it and see."

Mateo's grin spread across his handsome face as he reached up and gave one of her curls a tug. The tug only served to make Kailyn giggle. When she threw her head back in laughter at the second tug, Mateo captured her lips. The world tilted off its axis as he pulled her close, deepened the kiss, and caused the temperature between them both to rise a few degrees.

EPILOGUE

Most people had favorite colors. His birth mother's favorite color had been red on account of a doll. His adoptive mother's favorite had been mahogany, which was reddish brown.

For years, Aldo had thought Tessa Matthews loved that color because of a film starring her favorite actress which she'd watch at least once a month on the old television in the family room. At her funeral, he'd learned that his second mother had fallen in love with the color after her husband planted a hibiscus shrub as a border around her garden.

The bush still thrived there today. Its reddish-brown foliage had never held Aldo's attention like it did for his twin brother Mateo. Whenever Mateo encountered anything with red, he usually treated it like a stoplight and came to a halt and stared at it with a stupid grin on his face.

Aldo didn't have a favorite color. But he did have a favorite letter. It was the letter M. The beginning of his new last name, which had given him a fresh start in life.

He liked the curves that made up the top of the letter. The symmetry of the form was pleasing to his eyes. Maybe another reason Aldo liked the shape of the M because there were two curves in the letter—twin peaks.

Just as he reached the summit of one side, he would arrive in a valley and look up to see another mountain to climb. Though sometimes the twin mountains would flatten out, compressing into a thin line. He didn't like it when that happened. Other times, the mountains would smoosh together, making the distance between them closer and the valley non-existent. In his mind, he thought of stretching his body out across the twin peaks. Maybe even tasting both summits at the same time.

"Are you even listening to me?"

Aldo blinked. He jerked his attention up. Way up past the purse of her top lip. Up beyond the flare of her nostrils. Higher to the blaze of those bright green eyes.

There, he had to pause. It always took him at least two seconds before he could orient himself in her gaze. Having Elayne Jade's full attention on him always made Aldo feel hot under his collar. The steam from that heat would fog up his brain.

He had to be careful because in those few moments, she could get the better of him. And if she got the better of him, he would be the one to lose in the game they had played since they were children. They game of who could make the other pop their top.

Aldo was the reigning champion of the game. With just a few well-placed words, he could rile Elayne up enough that those perfectly shaped lips would part, forming the most exquisite M shape he could ever imagine.

"I don't know what game you're playing at, Aldo Matthews, but I'm going to make you regret it."

Her lips parted slightly. But the shape was all

wrong. The right side of her mouth lifted higher than the left side, making the shape off balance. He needed to find the right words to irritate her enough to get them back in alignment.

"You think I could regret anything more than finding myself hitched to you?" He hurled the words at her. And bingo! Her lips parted, but only briefly, before she huffed out an angry breath that made them bow a bit.

"Well, there's an easy fix to that."

Aldo felt something thump against his chest. At first, he didn't react to it. His heart often beat rapidly around Elayne Jade. It was the thrill of the game they played, and he knew he was winning.

"Just sign the annulment papers."

Her mouth compressed into a flat line as she breathed through her nose. Uh-oh. He was losing. The mountains were disappearing in the horizon of her face.

Victory had been so close. Where had he gone wrong?

Aldo looked down at the papers she had thrust at him. In bold black letters, he saw words across the top. One word stood out to him.

Annulment.

Aldo recoiled at the word as though it were a snake weaving through his tranquil valley. That word had no place here. It did not belong between them.

"Well? What are you waiting for?" Elayne was saying. "You want to be rid of me, don't you? Sign the papers."

She flung the pages at him, but Aldo refused to catch them. Why would he? This was not what he wanted. This was not how he wanted to play the game. He had been so close to winning. Now it felt like he was not just losing this match, it felt like he might never win with her again.

The pages slipped free and cascaded down to the floor with abandon. Aldo saw why. The paper-clip that had held them came loose and was now caught in Elayne's hair.

Without thinking, he reached up to snag the metallic clip. When he did so, his fingertips brushed against Elayne's cheek. Her lips parted on a sharp inhale. His gaze was immediately drawn to her mouth, where he saw it—two perfect twin peaks.

Climbing was the last thing on his mind. Conquering was what he wanted to do. Aldo wanted to take that perfectly shaped M and capture it in his mouth. He wanted to plunge into the valley between her top lip to find the treasure buried there. For the first time, he realized that was the prize in this game that they played.

If he won, which he had every intention of doing, then he could kiss Elayne Jade's perfect mouth.

A sound from across the hall jerked her attention away from him. Elayne blew out a long, low breath that she must have been holding. The exhalation compressed her lips, flattening the mountain Aldo had been about to conquer.

She pulled away from his hold before he could close his hands around her nape. The papers swished and crumpled under her feet as she stormed off. His first instinct was to give chase, but there was no need. He already had her cornered. He just needed to bide his time before he came out the inevitable victor.

Oh boy!

I think you can see the writing on the wall with Elayne and Aldo.

Are you ready for an enemies to lovers romance?

But I don't think these two are true enemies...
Get caught up in the whirlwind of their unexpected
romance in
"His Vow to Defend,"
the final book in the Flying Cross Ranch Romances!

Shanae Johnson was raised by Saturday Morning cartoons and After School Specials. She still doesn't understand why there isn't a life lesson that ties the issues of the day together just before bedtime. While she's still waiting for the meaning of it all, she writes stories to try and figure it all out. Her books are wholesome and sweet, but her are heroes are hot and heroines are full of sass!

And by the way, the E elongates the A. So it's pronounced Shan-aaaaaaaa. Perfect for a hero to call out across the moors, or up to a balcony, or to blare outside her window on a boombox. If you hear him calling her name, please send him her way!

You can sign up for Shanae's Reader Group and receive a FREE NOVELLA in this world at

https://shanaejohnson.com/ReaderGroup

ALSO BY SHANAE JOHNSON

a Flying Cross Ranch Romance

His Vow to Love

His Vow to Treasure

His Vow to Adore

His Vow to Trust

His Vow to Respect

His Vow to Defend

The Silver Star Ranch Romances

His Pledge to Honor

His Pledge to Cherish

His Pledge to Protect

His Pledge to Obey

His Pledge to Have

His Pledge to Hold

The Brides of Purple Heart

On His Bended Knee

Hand Over His Heart

Offering His Arm

His Permanent Scar

Having His Back

In Over His Head

Always On His Mind

Every Step He Takes

In His Good Hands

Light Up His Life

Strength to Stand

His Grace Under Pressure

The Rangers of Purple Heart

The Rancher takes his Convenient Bride

The Rancher takes his Best Friend's Sister

The Rancher takes his Runaway Bride

The Rancher takes his Star Crossed Love

The Rancher takes his Love at First Sight

The Rancher takes his Last Chance at Love